# THE
# COLLECTIVE

# THE COLLECTIVE

## LINDSEY WHITLOCK

Pushkin Press
71–75 Shelton Street
London WC2H 9JQ

*The Collective* was first published in Great Britain
by Pushkin Press in 2019

3 5 7 9 8 6 4 2

ISBN 13: 978-1-78269-217-1

Designed and typeset by Tetragon, London
Printed and bound by CPI Group (UK) Ltd, Croydon, CR0 4YY

www.pushkinpress.com

# THE
# COLLECTIVE

# ILLINOIS TERRITORY,
# COLLECTIVE HOMESTEADS OF AMERICA

# CHAPTER 1

## *Pigeon Spring*

THE YEAR ELWYN left home was a Pigeon Spring in Badfish Creek. Every seven years, the birds would come, darkening the sky like a plague of Egypt. But this was the New World, not the Old. The birds didn't bring fear or destruction. The birds brought excitement, like a coming storm. The hunting equipment wasn't the best; everyone used what they had. A lucky few carried shotguns. The rest carried slings, arrows, throwing sticks. Nets stretched from tree to tree. They filled with birds like bugs fill a screen, while children carried baskets around their necks and caught the birds as they fell from the sky. The filled baskets were dumped into a wagon, and the wagon was carried to Kegonsa, where the birds were gutted and bled and shipped by train south-west to St Louis and east along the Laurentian cities as far as Philadelphia.

They got three dollars for every bird, and the feeling of wealth poured into town before the money did. That summer, people would build homes, pay off debts, get married. For years, the forest floor would be fertile, fertile enough to grow the pumpkins whose vines were trained to climb the cottonwoods where the shade wasn't strong.

That first year, the pumpkins would grow so large, they would need to be held up with ropes.

It was a Pigeon Spring, and Badfish Creek ignited with excitement as the first shots were fired, and the sky grew darker and darker with fluttering bodies. Elwyn's arm whirled, his sling hurling stones that felled four passenger pigeons at a time, just like his father had taught him, and his father before him, and his father before that, on and on back seven generations to Samuel Bramble, one of the rebel slaves who fought in the Second American War before settling down in Badfish Creek among French mountain men and misfits. But even though Elwyn's ears were full of the roar of wings, even though the birds dropped from the sky, even though the thrill of the hunt was pumping through his body, below all that, Elwyn felt a restlessness. The restlessness had been growing all winter, maybe all his life.

When the last birds were shipped, men and women jumped into the still-icy creek to rinse the sweat, blood and feathers from their bodies. Children were washed in basins of warm well-water and oak bark; brothers and sisters with all shades of pale and dark young skin stood gleaming while they waited to be inspected by their mothers. Everyone was vigorously dried, believing wet ears meant illness, and wet feet drew bad spirits. Then as the sun went down and the bonfires were lit, people gathered close, wrapped in blankets and coats, roasting game as they always did, and singing and playing, flirting, minding babies. On that celebratory day, many bottles were opened and passed. Old Finchy opened a cask of the mead she was famous for as the singing grew louder and more joyful, more boisterous. Children played late into the night while young mothers nursed and got a chance to dream, for once, of the things they would buy.

While Badfish Creek celebrated its fortune, Elwyn wasn't with the others. Instead, he was alone in his room – an unusual thing for a boy who normally revelled in festival atmospheres. Like the other Badfishians, his head was full of dreams, but they were dreams of a different quality. In the light of a candle, his pen flew across the page, but no matter how fast Elwyn wrote, his hand couldn't keep up with words racing through his mind. He kept making mistakes, having to restart. He wanted the letter to be as great as the ambitions rising in him. He wanted it to be perfect. It was possible that this one letter, addressed to an aunt he had never spoken to, in a town he had never visited, could change the course of his whole life. And perhaps it did.

It was a letter asking his Aunt Piety if he could come and live with her. He sent it first thing the next morning, and for weeks after, Elwyn's life hinged on visits to the post office, where he checked in once, twice, sometimes three times a day to see if anything had arrived for him; there were no home deliveries in that part of the Collective, and the train that carried mail was unreliable. Elwyn's mood rose and fell with these visits, with the shake of Postman Wilder's head. And every day, it seemed more important to Elwyn that the letter arrive, not less. He realised that leaving Badfish Creek – leaving soon, making something of himself – was the pivotal thing, was what his life had been building towards.

But as often happens, the day the letter arrived was the one day Elwyn neglected his morning visit to the post office – his brother Allun had convinced him the morning would be better spent out fishing; the bass were biting. Later, hungry from the fresh air and industry, Elwyn sat at the kitchen table reading a book and eating acorn bread while his mother swept the floor. When Mirth Bramble cleaned, her arms looked like the legs of a draught horse: strong, deliberate. Crumbs fell down around Elwyn as he read, but for once, Mirth didn't seem to see them. She glanced at the small stack of mail on the counter and then back at her son. After a few minutes, she stopped sweeping and took an envelope from the pile.

'I stopped in at the post office earlier. This came for you,' she said, handing it to Elwyn. She went back to sweeping. He saw her glance over at him as he examined the crisp paper and the address written in a practised hand. His fingers shook a little as he unfolded the enclosed letter. As he did, a smile grew on his face. Happiness seemed to spread over his entire body, radiate from him. When he was done reading, he set the letter aside and took another bite of bread, a bite of self-satisfaction.

'So, what did she say?' Mirth asked in a too-casual voice, not looking up.

'It's not from Aunt Piety. It's from her husband. He says I can stay with them.'

Mirth poked at the dust behind the stove.

'Well, you are nearly sixteen,' she said. 'You can make your own decisions.'

Elwyn nodded, brushing crumbs of bread from the table back onto his plate and tipping them into his mouth.

'Of course I can,' he said with a wink.

'Elwyn. . .' his mother began. 'I don't think you know what you're getting into.'

'I thought you said I was old enough to make my own decisions,' he teased.

'I grew up in Hill Country, Elwyn. I know there are a lot of advantages to the education you can get in a place like Liberty. I know there are opportunities, and that can seem exciting. But you are still a boy. You are used to being known. Liked. Understood. It won't be like that living with my sister. It won't be like that with those people. I think you underestimate how difficult the path forward will be for you. It's very different in Liberty than it is here, Elwyn.'

'That's why I want to go.' He put his plate in the wash basin and kissed his mother on her cheek. Her muscles were tense. 'Oh, don't worry so much, Mam. I'll be all right – I always am. I plan on coming back, you know. And coming back rich. And then I'll buy you a big house. And *dozens* of brooms,' he said, laughing as he patted her on the back. She sighed heavily, but her muscles loosened slightly. Elwyn went to the door and put on his hat.

'Where are you going?' said Mirth.

'Going to tell Whim. She's got good paper. I'll write the letter there and take it to the post office on my way back. I've got to let the Blackwells know when I'm coming,' he said before leaving.

The spring air smelt fresh to him for the first time in years. Later, when he returned home, Elwyn would fold that letter from his uncle carefully back into its envelope and put it with the others he had received from Liberty – all from his aunt, mostly Christmas cards. They had started coming when he was four and stopped by the time he was twelve. He kept them in a small wooden box under his bed, where he kept all the things that were his and only his: a coin, an arrowhead, a few maps clipped from newspapers.

# CHAPTER 2

# *Whim*

BADFISH CREEK wasn't a place used to change. Deep in the Illinois Territory, it had been settled shortly after the Second War by a group of what came to be called Foresters: a mix of fur-hunters, anarchists and a handful of rebel slaves that had abandoned the land they had been bound to. That was 1820, when the Foresters committed to building their houses around trunks of trees, never borrowing money, and never tilling the earth.

Elwyn's leaving caused no small stir in the community. Everyone had an opinion, and in the months before he set off, they seemed to talk of nothing else. *It's what comes of marrying outsiders*, was a common whisper (Elwyn's late father had been a handsome, well-liked person, the sort of man a town hates to see marry anyone but their own daughters). The older women, with their lace and superstitions, said it was Elwyn's mother's fault for bundling him in too many blankets and keeping the windows closed during his infant naps. But Elwyn had supporters, too. His older brother Allun, who was engaged and feeling the squeeze of responsibility, thought it was prudent to make a little money while young. Teilo, the youngest brother, hoped

Elwyn would send back some livestock he could keep as pets. And the distiller, Aelred, was also a surprising ally. His daughter Whim and Elwyn had been friends for most of their childhood. Aelred thought it was time they went their separate ways.

For his part, Elwyn didn't pay much attention to other people's opinions. It was said that he looked like his father's line, and Elwyn liked to think he also had their free-minded ways. That spring he did what he always did: hunted and read and made mild mischief. If there was any difference, it was only the unquenchable light of possibility he carried inside him. His other brothers and sisters spent what remained of their time together teasing him about going to Hill Country, but this only added to the pleasure of his preparations. He was the fourth of seven children; teasing wasn't anything he wasn't used to.

'But, Elwyn, why can't you just study at home? Why would you want to go to *Liberty*?' his sister Enid said as they sat up in a branch of an oak with their slings, waiting for a cottontail. 'It sounds so boring! Stiff and prim and proper. And Mam says Aunt Piety was always so strange and serious. You want to live with someone like that?'

Elwyn shrugged. He thought he saw a rabbit behind a nearby tree and stood to get a better look.

'I mean, we all know you like a challenge. But going to *Hill Country*, Elwyn? It sounds terrible. And leaving us all. Leaving *Whim*. How can you leave her? The two of you are practically an old married couple already.'

'We're friends, Enid,' Elwyn said, slightly annoyed. His sister had spoken too loudly, the rabbit had slipped away. Or maybe it was just staying still, hiding. He moved to another branch to get a better view. 'This is an opportunity.'

'An opportunity. Ha! I can just see you with those stuffy old Hill people, your collar buttoned high, sipping your tea.' Enid imitated her image of him, eyes laughing, but Elwyn was standing still, waiting for any movement from under the dogwood bush. Enid scrunched her nose, plucked an old acorn, and shot it at his shoulder.

'Elwyn, you know I can't stand people who don't pay attention to me while I make fun of them!'

Elwyn took another acorn and threw it back at her with a sly grin, jumping down from the tree.

'Hey! That hurt!' Enid said, but she was grinning and already running after him, another acorn in her hand. Below the trees, green things were pushing up in all the familiar ways. Inside Elwyn, there was nothing but readiness.

Or so it was until his last night in Badfish Creek. That night, Elwyn had intended to sleep well. The days were lengthening and the air was warm. While the rest of the town was out for a 'good wrestle with this spring air', as they used to say, Elwyn was climbing into bed. He shut his eyes, but sleep didn't find him. Even though he could hear laughter from outside the window – kids playing tip-the-tin and mothers gossiping – the room was still unnaturally quiet without his four brothers breathing and turning in their sleep.

At first Elwyn thought it was their absence that kept him up. But one by one, the boys found their way to their beds like foxes to their den, and the usual hum of their night-time noises returned to the little room. Elwyn still lay awake in bed. He lay, and he lay. The music and chatter faded. The night grew deeper, quieter. He still couldn't sleep.

And then he understood. Long after stillness had settled over Badfish Creek, Elwyn threw off his sheets and crept into the forest, stepping over the wood violets and through the nettles to the creek, a book under his arm.

Along the bank, a house made of river stones was huddled on the earth. Rabbits nibbled on young lettuce and a few ducks pecked in the yard. Elwyn walked along the path until he arrived at Whim's house. He knocked on her window.

'Whim? Whim Moone? Are you awake?'

He waited a moment and knocked again.

'Whi—'

She was there. She opened the window.

'Sorry, I didn't hear you. You are always so quiet,' he said.

'It's the middle of the night.' Her eyes were bleary with sleep.

'I forgot to return this to you,' he said, holding out the book. She looked at it blankly for a moment, then back at him. Elwyn felt her reading his face. She seemed to know how to read everything.

'Do you want to talk about something?' she asked.

He didn't have to reply. Whim wrapped herself in a coat and climbed out the window without a sound that could be heard above the pickerel frogs and grey tree frogs singing in the reeds. She sat beside Elwyn on the bank, and they watched the moon on the water, reflecting off her pale face and his dark one. He pulled a little cloth pouch of shelled walnuts from his pocket, and set it between them to share while they talked – a tradition of theirs that neither of them could remember the beginning of. Whim took some, keeping her eyes on Elwyn all the while.

'I leave for the Blackwells' tomorrow,' he said.

'I know. You've talked about it all spring.'

'But I was wrong, Whim.'

'Wrong about what?'

'I was wrong thinking I could go without you.'

Whim looked at him, reading, again, but Elwyn didn't want to be distracted.

'You're my best friend. We haven't been apart for more than a couple of days since we were six. What am I going to do without you there?' he said. Whim looked away and half-smiled, but it was an amused sort of smile that irritated Elwyn. 'Don't do that,' he said.

'What did you think would happen when you went away, Elwyn? I can't magically appear at your side whenever you want some company.'

'Oh, I don't know. You know how I can be sometimes.'

'I do.'

'Whim. I want you to come with me.'

'To Liberty? Elwyn, you're going tomorrow.'

'I've thought it through—'

'Elwyn.'

'Okay, maybe I haven't thought it through completely. But just think about it. You don't need to come now. Take some time. Talk to your father, pack your bags, do whatever needs to be done. Then come. Get on the train. Come find me.'

Whim was quiet, a bit of the amused smile still standing on her lips. But maybe there was a bit of wistfulness, too. Elwyn thought he saw it around the edges of her eyes, and it encouraged him.

'Come in a week. Or two. Or three. Whenever you can. Just come. There's a whole world out there for us, Whim. You're twice as smart as I am. You could do anything. *We* could do anything, Whim. And then someday we can come back to Badfish Creek, come back together, with some money in our pockets, having actually *done* something.'

'Elwyn—'

'I know. I know what everyone is saying. But, there's this whole world out there. It might not be perfect, but it's *ours*. Don't you want to even see it? Run around in it? Don't you want any of it?'

The wistful look grew on her face for a moment, like the moon grows.

'Of course I want it, Elwyn. Some of it.'

'You could paint cities. Find new plants. Read all kinds of books, thousands of books. We could do it together. The two of us. Out in the world.' Elwyn felt young and alive as he smiled at Whim. She called it his 'impossible smile' because he made it so impossible not to smile back. But this time she didn't. She just sighed and looked at the water.

'Elwyn, you're my best friend—' she began with the care and intelligence that was so natural to her.

'And you're mine—'

'But you know that I can't come with you.' There was something honest in the way Whim spoke. It was as familiar to Elwyn as the trillium that still grew on the cool side of the creek.

'Why?'

'Not with Mother gone.'

'That was ten years ago, Whim. I know your dad isn't crazy about me. But he loves you. He'll come around. He'll understand. I can't let you just stay here, trapped in the same life, doing the same things year after year. Stuck someplace where only this tiny sliver of things are possible for you.'

'I'm all he has, Elwyn. And this place is all any of us have.'

Elwyn looked down. He picked at the dirt with his finger. 'I wish you weren't such a good person, sometimes.'

They were quiet. The space between them seemed to grow.

'Do you remember when we were kids? We said we'd buy Old Finchy's house together,' Elwyn said. 'I'd get the right side, you'd get the left.'

'And you had plans to build a toboggan run from the roof for winter, and a swinging rope for summer. Just because Finchy would hate it,' Whim said.

'We always promised we'd do everything together.'

'You're the one who's leaving, Elwyn,' Whim said. The wistfulness had left her eyes. Elwyn opened his mouth, but he found he didn't have anything he could say.

'We aren't kids any more,' Whim went on, looking out at the creek. 'We each have our place in the world, Elwyn. We need to take the course laid out for us.'

That was something Elwyn didn't believe, not even a little. But he knew that when Whim got philosophical, the conversation was over. Elwyn picked himself up off the riverbank, unsettled and unhappy. But when he arrived back home, he slept well. And he woke the next day with only a shadow of regret and the full lightness of that unquenchable feeling that his life was just beginning.

# CHAPTER 3

# Bird and Badger

THAT NIGHT, Whim dreamt that the passenger pigeons returned. Only they weren't passenger pigeons at all. They were locusts, covering the town, devouring everything. And in the dream, while woods were being eaten by the insects, Elwyn was walking away. Whim could see him, and she called and she called, but no matter how many times she yelled his name, he never heard her. He never turned around.

She woke long after dawn, which she never did. That day of all days. With a sense of urgency, she pulled on her long coat and ran outside, past the budding gardens, a honking herd of Canada geese. The familiar faces of people tending plots or taking their sewing outside turned to ask where she was going. She didn't stop for any of them. Corker's bicycle, the only bike in town, was leaning against a tree. She hopped on and started to peddle away, yelling back to Corker that she would pay him later. He charged half a penny a ride.

The bicycle was rickety and the six-mile road from Badfish Creek to the Kegonsa train station was riddled with roots and rocks. Whim's jaw rattled as she peddled faster and faster, hoping desperately that she could make it there before Elwyn's train left. She felt deep in her bones that something was about to happen. That Elwyn needed to stay.

The train was already at the station. Whim dropped the bicycle and ran onto the platform, scanning the station for him, then scanning the train's windows. Her heart was in her throat. The roar of the locusts in her dream was still in her ears. Everything else was a blur, everything but the shape of Elwyn's face, which she caught sight of through the dirty window of the passenger car.

Elwyn noticed Whim moments after she noticed him. But when Elwyn turned towards her and his eyes brightened, Whim's heart lurched. She swore it actually leapt out of her, tearing her chest as it reached towards Elwyn. And then her heart returned to its place. The packed-dirt station and the few people around it came into focus. Whim came into focus herself. And she knew, then, that she couldn't ask him to stay. She had only had a dream. It just seemed urgent because it was about Elwyn. And she wanted him to stay. So much.

Elwyn smiled as he opened his window and leant out. He was on the sunny side of the train, and the sun seemed to shine on him especially. That was the way it was with Elwyn. Being around him felt like standing in the sun.

'You changed your mind,' he said, grinning.

Whim shook her head, swallowed hard, and forced a smile. 'No. I just came to say goodbye.'

Elwyn's face fell, but only a little. The gleam was still there, the shine. In Badfish Creek, people said Elwyn was born twice-lucky: he was born in May, the luckiest month, and he was born a dark-skinned boy to two pale parents. This, according to the older Foresters, was a mark of good fortune. Elwyn had never put much stock in that; the younger generation wasn't so attached to old wives' tales. But as Elwyn leant out the window, Whim thought maybe he *had* been born lucky. Not because of the month of his birth or the colour of his skin, but because of the unquenchable optimism that seemed to dwell inside him.

'Mam wouldn't let anyone come down to the station with me. She said there was enough fuss already, and too much work to be done. You know how she is about goodbyes. Only Teilo snuck down.' Elwyn waved to his youngest brother, who was sitting quietly on the dirt platform with his pet chicken, a runaway from some distant farm. Teilo was a reticent kid and didn't wave back. Elwyn chuckled.

Further down the train, the conductor carried a final crate onto the freight car. In it were deer pelts, barrels and a few bottles. Whim realised she could jump in after the crate was on, before the conductor closed the door of the freight car. She could hide behind the crates, peek through the holes to see when they arrived in Liberty. She could send word with Teilo that she had gone. Her father would be heartbroken, but he would find his own way in the world. Maybe we all needed to find our own ways in the world. Maybe Elwyn was right.

But Whim didn't believe that. She believed that we are bound to each other, by strings of love and duty. The moment passed, and the conductor closed the door.

'I've got something for you,' Elwyn said. He stretched it out to her, his body half out the window. It was his favourite sling. Whim reached up and took it, her fingers not touching his. She looked at Elwyn quizzically.

'I packed my old one, but I figure I'm not going to need two any more,' he said. 'It's all books and business and proper stuff like that for me now. For a while anyway. And who knows? You might run across some Goliath that needs slaying.' Elwyn's eyes twinkled teasingly. Whim knew Elwyn thought it was funny to think of her in any sort of battle, peacemaker that she was. 'Besides, if I leave it at home, Dewey will get ahold of it, and he loses everything,' he laughed 'You'll take care of it?'

'Of course.'

'You'll practise using it?' he said, this time with a wink.

'That I can't promise.' Whim smiled almost sincerely.

The train began to pull away. Whim started to walk alongside Elwyn's window, as if she were tied to it.

'If you change your mind, Whim, you know where I'll be,' Elwyn said, his smile broadening as the train picked up speed. 'Come and find me!' he shouted before he turned away from her to face the wind. And then, in only a minute, he was gone. Out of sight.

The loud train left a hush over the station. The station-master, also Kegonsa's store-owner and innkeeper, swept the dust that settled in the train's wake. The comfortable sounds of bristles on a dirt path, the click of two men playing checkers under the store's eaves, the strange little throat sounds of Teilo's chicken: these familiar noises were an unspeakable comfort at a moment that seemed to tear Whim apart. And as always, there was the sound of the trees. The sound of the wind stirring leaves as loud and constant as a river.

'Do you want to ride home?' Whim said. Teilo was only six and still a little round in the cheeks. He didn't say anything as he hopped on the back of Corker's bike.

'Do you think Elwyn will buy me a cow when he's rich?' Teilo surprised Whim by asking when they were about halfway home. Whim was wiping stray tears from her eyes.

'What would a cow eat in the woods?' Whim managed.

'Acorns.'

When Whim returned home, she was surprised to find her father Aelred there, with a late breakfast set on the table and a little bouquet of wood violets in the centre. They were the flowers her father always said reminded him of her; they were quiet, but fragrant, and did everyone some good.

He didn't ask where she had gone. But when they had sat and begun to eat, he looked up at her and spoke.

'You are a bird, little Whim. Singing your songs. Building your nest. He's a badger. Made for wandering widely, building burrows and abandoning them.'

'I know what I am,' Whim said. 'But sometimes, just for a little while, I wish I could be something else.'

# CHAPTER 4

# *Liberty*

ELWYN HAD SEEN LIBERTY BEFORE, but not in person. A moving panorama show once came through the forest towns, setting up in the main room of the Kegonsa station, the only place big enough. Heavy shades were drawn, and a light shone on a massive painting that moved between two scrolls. It seemed as long as the creek itself.

Everyone scraped together money to go. It was collected by the young boy who turned the crank that moved the scrolls. A man with oiled hair and crooked teeth spoke in a musical voice about the images that passed by. The panoramas of natural disasters were the most popular: a hurricane over Carolina sea islands; double tornadoes on the Laurentian Lakes; the grass fire on the Flatlands. And there was also the mile-wide Messipi, a natural wonder near enough that the Badfishians felt some ownership of it, though none of them had ever travelled there. People talked about these images for weeks.

The panorama show never came back to the woods. Maybe it was too hard to lug the giant scrolls down overgrown roads, or maybe the showman was a part-time crook disappointed to find everyone's pockets empty. But the images stayed with Elwyn. If he'd had the money, he would have watched the show over and over, sitting open-eyed and perfectly still in the darkness. There had been a few brief scenes of the Hill towns along the Wisconsin river, including Liberty. The railroad and riverboat traffic made them popular getaways for moneyed Messipi traders and old Franco-Indian merchant families; they said that the ancient rocks and soil were good for people's health. Some of the Foresters had booed those images and jeered the man to move on to something more exciting. But Elwyn still remembered the wide stone streets, the shops built into the hillsides, the horses pulling carts. There was a grassy park by the river with a single tree and several benches, and everything appeared so tidy and prosperous and pretty. That was Liberty. That was where his aunt lived.

Elwyn looked eagerly out the windows of the train as it neared town. Bicycles sped down streets, horses trotted ahead of wagons, white steamboats chugged along the river. Everything was moving. It pulled at him almost physically – he felt that if the window weren't there he would lean so far forward, he'd tumble right out onto the grass.

The train arrived at Liberty Station an hour late, and Elwyn practically jumped out of his seat onto the platform. He was carrying a large cake box and dressed in the starched, many-buttoned clothes purchased by his mother. His shirt was the pale green of coneflower dye with a stiff bow at the neck, and it was unlike anything he saw worn by the people there. As he wandered through the crowd, people turned to look at Elwyn. It wasn't just his clothes they were staring at, it was all of him, from his way of moving to his hair to the shade of his skin. The people in Liberty were almost all pale, pale even compared to people like Elwyn's mother, who had darkened after years in the sun. He made an effort to stand tall and be lively as he searched for his aunt and uncle. But he felt uncomfortable in the gaze of the people passing by, and discomfort wasn't a feeling Elwyn was used to.

He could not find his aunt and uncle on the platform, so juggling the cake box and slinging his deerskin bag, Elwyn went inside the station. At the far wall was a wooden bar where a few people sat on velvet stools and lunched. The thick air was redolent of roasted roots and beef. Elwyn's stomach growled; he had already eaten the salted game and acorn bread packed for the half-day's journey. *Someday, that will be me*, Elwyn thought. *Taking a break while I travel, sitting on a stool and eating steak and drinking beer.*

A man behind the bar was chatting with a customer and chewing a toothpick. Elwyn moved the cake box to his other arm.

'Excuse me?' Elwyn said. 'I'm Elwyn. Elwyn Bramble. Is there someone waiting for me?'

A few people glanced sidelong at Elwyn, then averted their eyes, but the man behind the bar looked from Elwyn's face to his clothes to the cake box tied with home-woven lace he held under one arm.

'The Blackwells?' Elwyn tried again, when the man said nothing. 'A man and a woman?'

'Farms have all the hands they need around here. Try again come harvest,' the man said.

'Oh, no. I'm not here to work on a farm. I'm here to learn. To study. Prepare for my future. I'm staying with my aunt, Piety Blackwell.'

The man moved the toothpick from one side of his mouth to the other and watched Elwyn through narrow eyes.

'Maybe you could give me directions,' Elwyn suggested. '1434 Citizen Street.'

'You're not in the right place.'

'This is Liberty Station, right? It says so on the sign,' Elwyn said.

The man took the toothpick out of his mouth and inspected the chewed end. 'I said, you're not in the right place.'

The people at the bar were staring at Elwyn. Normally, Elwyn was someone who liked attention, who thrived on the eyes of others. But this time the gazes made him shrink away. He became uncomfortably aware of the way he stood, the darkness of his skin, the bows on his clothes, the odd colour of the fabric.

'I'll go look someplace else, then,' Elwyn said cautiously.

They watched him as he stepped back out the door. The smell of hot grass was in the air, and hot metal and steam and smoke and stone. Elwyn shielded his eyes from the sun to look for his aunt and uncle once more before he ventured to find their house himself. The road was in front of him, as bright as before; the stones were hot below his feet. He hoisted the cake box onto his shoulder and began to walk.

1434 Citizen Street was an address Elwyn had known since he was a child, written on envelopes in his aunt's tiny lettering. He had read and re-read those old letters from Aunt Piety, entranced not just by their words, but the weight and whiteness of the paper, the smoothness of the ink, the sound of the address. Badfish Creek didn't have street names; there was something thrilling about the idea of towns with so many houses that people needed numbers to keep them straight. What an interesting place!

But Elwyn didn't know how to navigate by address. He turned down whichever streets looked the most promising and became distracted by shop windows full of shining cow-leather shoes, dark blue suits, tall cakes, copper pots, pens, greenhouse flowers, ice cream. It was wonderful and almost painful to see the possibilities strung together down the streets like pearls on a string. Bicycles sped past, and horses snorted. Men yelled from their carts for him to move out of the way.

It was all new to him, and as thrilling as it was disorienting. Elwyn was hot and hungry when he finally found his way to Citizen Street, way out on the west side of town.

It was quieter there, and he looked up at the wooden road sign with a flood of appreciation when he felt a tug at his sleeve. A ugly grey goat was behind him, making a snack of his shirt.

'Shoo,' Elwyn said. But the goat followed closely, nibbling the cloth where he could. By the time Elwyn reached the Blackwells' door, several buttons were missing and sweat pooled and dripped down his back.

The front door was white and, like the skylights and the windows, was built into the grassy hill in accordance with the old Hill custom. For generations, the house had belonged to his uncle's family, who Elwyn knew little about except that they were quite rich. He couldn't quite tell where the house ended. Little windows and skylights dappled the mown grass a long ways.

Elwyn was eager to see what was inside, and to meet the family he had thought so much about all these years. He knocked and tried to smooth his hair while he waited – everything around him was so trim and neat, it threw his own rumpled appearance into relief. He tried to catch his reflection in a window when the door opened. He had wondered if there would be a maid, but instead the door was answered by a boy about Elwyn's age. The boy had a pointed chin, a sour-looking mouth.

'Hello. Is this the Blackwells' house?' Elwyn said. The boy didn't answer, but as they stood there, Elwyn recognised something in the lines of the boy's nose and eyes that reminded him of his mother's. 'Are you Boaz?

My cousin?' Elwyn said, a smile spreading over his tired face. The boy's face was unchanged. 'I'm Elwyn. Elwyn Bramble. I've come to stay with you.'

Again, the boy just stood.

'Boaz? Who is it?' a man called from inside. 'You've been excused to leave the table, but manners dictate a prompt return.'

The boy slipped away, leaving the door open and disappearing somewhere into the halls. Elwyn followed. It took a while for Elwyn's eyes to adjust to the dim light of the under-hill house. The air was sweet with the smell of old paper, wool and wood polish, but there was something else in the air, too. Lunch. The thought of food consumed Elwyn, distracting him from the grandfather clocks, the portraits on the wall. He followed the smell.

'Boaz?' the voice called again, now louder.

'Let him be,' a woman said as Elwyn turned the corner into a dim dining room decorated with pewter and paintings. A bearded man sat at one end of the long table, his plate full of peas and butter, cheese and bread, white slices of chicken. At the other end, with a more modest plate, was a woman who could only be Aunt Piety. Her face was like Elwyn's mother's, but leaner, less worn. Her eyebrows arched as she looked at Elwyn, and he felt silly with his torn clothes and a large cake box in his arms, a cake he would have been tempted to try if he didn't fear the wrath of his mother.

'You're late,' the man said, shovelling a forkful of peas into his mouth. He had a rolling stomach and two stick-like legs tucked below the table. Glasses sat on a squat nose guarded by heavy jowls. 'You were due to come at noon.'

'The train was late.'

'To bow to the train's faulty schedule is to give in to chaos. Punctuality, you will come to understand, is strictly adhered to in this house.'

'Your uncle is very fond of schedules,' Aunt Piety said, leaning back in her chair. 'You can expect a proper greeting when mealtime ends in' – she looked up at the clock – 'thirty seconds.'

The man scowled, but buttered his bread, some crumbs falling into his beard as he ate. 'Quite right. For, how many times have I said it, Piety? Timeliness is the foundation of orderliness, and orderliness is the foundation of civility itself.'

Just then, several clocks clanged at once, all with different chimes. At that sound, the cook came in and began to clear plates. The man dabbed his face with a napkin before standing up and extending his hand.

'Now,' he said. 'Elwyn Bramble, I am Timothy Blackwell. You may call me Uncle, despite the obvious lack of blood relation. I'm pleased to meet you.' And he did look pleased, smiling at Elwyn, untroubled by or unaware of his nephew's unkempt appearance. Elwyn set the cake box down and shook his uncle's hand. 'In handshakes, always be firm, but never *too* firm, Nephew,'

Timothy corrected. 'An overly firm handshake is a sign of aggression. Aggression is a sign of weakness.' He saw some gesture imperceptible to Elwyn out of the corner of his eye and turned around to his wife. 'This is my project, Piety. How I instruct the boy is none of your concern.'

'I didn't say a thing,' she said, then turned to Elwyn, still in her seat, and extended her hand. 'I am Piety Blackwell, and that's what you may call me.' When he shook her hand, she said his handshake wasn't nearly firm enough, and he couldn't tell if she was joking.

'I brought you a cake,' Elwyn said. 'My mam sent it, to thank you. To thank you both.'

'What kind is it?' Piety had eyes that seemed to be reading everything – like Whim's, but much less forgiving.

'Not one I've ever had before. She said something about pepper-honey? She said you'd know.'

'Wasp cake,' Piety said, smiling, but not happily. 'It used to be a favourite of mine.'

'Your aunt doesn't eat sweets,' Timothy said, taking the cake box and handing it off to the maid. 'But you can write to your mother later and let her know that the gesture was greatly appreciated. It is, after all, the gesture that matters.'

'Timothy will surely appreciate it.' Piety nodded towards Timothy, who watched the cake leaving the room.

'All things in moderation,' Timothy said. Elwyn was also watching the cake and plates still full of chicken disappear. His stomach rumbled. 'Let me show you to your room, then we can get down to business at, say, quarter to five.'

'Do you think I can have something to eat first?'

'You will have to learn to listen more closely to conversation, Nephew. I think it has already been firmly established for you that mealtimes are to be strictly adhered to. This household, like all places of order and reason, has a schedule. You will soon learn it. But for now, the preliminary things. I have everything prepared for your lessons. Come along. I'll take your things.'

'Lessons? Won't school begin in the fall?' Elwyn asked. But his uncle had already picked up Elwyn's buckskin bag. Timothy held it far from his body as though it held a hive, and gestured with his other hand that Elwyn follow him out into the hall.

As Elwyn left the room, he turned back to look at his aunt. The grey eyes were watching him, her hands folded before her. Whim said you could tell everything you want to know about a person by looking at their hands and their eyes. Piety's hands were pale and unworked, that was easy enough to see. But as for her eyes, Elwyn thought at first that they looked bored, but the next moment he thought they were laughing.

# CHAPTER 5

# *Devotion*

THE BLACKWELL HOUSE was an old place. It had winding halls, deep closets and narrow, skylit rooms. The idea of building houses into hills had originally been a humble impulse, but wealthy families like Timothy Blackwell's soon discovered an advantage: when ostentatiousness is out of fashion, it's handy to have a home whose size no one can see. And the Blackwell house, bought generations ago with Blackwell money, was a sprawling, well-kept place. For over a hundred years, the floors had been trod on and cleaned and waxed. The clocks were kept wound, faces clean.

The strangest thing about the house, Elwyn discovered, was that it was divided in two. The original owners, husband and wife, often quarrelled, and so they made every arrangement to live as separately as possible while retaining respectability. This tradition, it seemed, had either been maintained or renewed, because one half of the house was clearly Piety's, the other was Timothy's, with the dining room and a formal parlour in the middle. Timothy gave a quick tour, naming the rooms as they passed them: Piety's study, Piety's bedroom, Piety's sitting room. Piety's library,

Piety's parlour. There were fewer clocks in her side of the house, different paintings, different sorts of books.

The house was not what Elwyn had imaged. He had been told that his mother and his aunt had both left the Hill farm where they had grown up, his mother to marry his father, his aunt to get an education. Mirth had wound up poor, while Piety married into a rich old family. Rich. Elwyn had pictured her house as a place with crystal chandeliers. Gold leaf on the wallpaper. Velvet cushions, silk pillows. Instead, there were clocks. And rugs. And rooms. Sturdy antique furniture wet with polish. They were, in fact, fine things, but not the sort Elwyn knew how to value, and he was vaguely disappointed.

Elwyn's room was in Timothy's half of the house, the northern side, where less sun slanted through the heavy glass. It was an austere room with a well-built desk, a well-built bed, thick sheets. If anything, it was plainer than the rest of the house, but stepping inside, Elwyn felt overwhelmingly grateful. He had never had a room all to himself.

'A bath has been drawn for you in the washroom down the hall,' Timothy said. 'Be sure to be at my study at exactly half past four. No later.' His heavily browed eyes looked over his glasses at Elwyn. 'Remember, Nephew: punctuality is the foundation of orderliness and—'

'"Orderliness is the foundation of civility". I remember,' Elwyn said, opening the wide armoire doors and putting the few things he had inside. Then he bathed and dressed and went where he was told. The airless little study was not far from Elwyn's room. He sat in a heavy chair as his uncle selected books from the shelves that covered the small space. The room smelt of those books; most of them were thick with unintelligible names like *Critical and Theoretical Underpinnings of Pedagogical Epistemologies.*

On the wall across from Elwyn was a large clock, its pendulum as long as his arm. In the glass face, Elwyn could see his own reflection. There was only one small mirror at his house in Badfish Creek, and Elwyn's sisters had pilfered it up to their room years ago. He found excuses to go up there and admire his face, the strong line of his jaw, his lively expressions. His sisters were constantly teasing him for it, but he didn't mind much; nothing was wrong with a little vanity where it was deserved. But even though his reflection looked just the same there in the study as it did in the mirror back home, something about it wasn't right. There was a dissonance.

Timothy closed the book he was perusing, cleaned his glasses and smiled. 'Let's get right to the core of it, Elwyn.' The look on his face was that of someone about to give a gift. 'Not only have I given you permission to stay here and offered to supervise your schooling – I have decided to *devote* myself to it. Your education will be my particular project. But it will require a great deal from you. It will require your full attention. Full devotion.'

'Devotion to what?'

'Attention, Nephew. *Devotion*. You will need to decide if you want to commit to this now. Because if you are unwilling, there is no point in our going any further.'

'I'm sorry – further in what?'

'In this project. *Our* project.' Timothy's jowls shook with emphasis. He didn't seem annoyed. He looked happy to have the opportunity explain himself, his work. Timothy lifted a notebook. 'Do you see this?' he asked. Elwyn nodded. 'This is where I will be keeping notes on our progress. *June the third*,' he read. '*Elwyn arrives. Appearance: dishevelled. Vocabulary: moderate. Introduction to instruction begun*.' Elwyn looked blankly at his uncle.

'You see, I used to work in academia. Social and educational research. I was working on studies that asked schools to incorporate the agricultural population by mandating that rural students be brought into schools in town centres three days a week. A highly successful experiment. It had been thought by many that it couldn't be done, that poor rural people shouldn't be given the same education as our more privileged citizens. My analysis countered that assumption and became quite sought after, not only within academia, but in government as well. For a while I was getting invitations to speak nearly every week. . .' Timothy's eyes glistened behind their thick spectacles, but then the gleam faded.

'That was all before my heart gave out – strain and overwork, you see. I was encouraged to take an early retirement. And of course it was a blessing. I had been putting off starting a family for quite some time. I met your aunt, we settled here in my old family home in Liberty – a fine town, quite sought after. I now have time to get involved in civic leadership – planning commission, education initiatives and so forth. And ample time for leisure.' Elwyn's uncle said this last word with barely veiled displeasure.

'But,' Timothy continued, 'when your letter arrived, it all became very clear. Why not get back into my old research? Take it a step further? If rural Hill folk could be educated, why not Foresters? I could write a first-hand account of it, of our work here, our success. An account of what a young Forester may become, given the proper guidance and instruction.' Uncle Timothy looked down at his notebook with tenderness, as though it were a child. 'The university will be clamouring to have me back,' he added, more to himself than to Elwyn. Then he looked up. 'Do you understand any of this?'

'I don't know,' Elwyn said, truthfully. He was a little light-headed with hunger.

'Well,' Timothy said, brightness returned to him, 'all I need to know from you is: are you willing to do what is necessary? To surmount any obstacles that come in your way? To devote yourself fully to your success?'

'Of course I am,' Elwyn said. 'I give myself fully to everything.' Timothy wrote something down in his notebook.

'That's what success is really about, right?' Elwyn went on. 'It isn't being good at what you do. It's about throwing yourself into something. And then the next thing and then the next until something sticks.'

But Timothy was scribbling away in his notebook and didn't seem to hear his nephew at all; Elwyn's attitude was hardly one his uncle would have agreed with. 'Now, the first step on the road to an educated life,' Timothy said, finishing what he was writing and closing the notebook, 'is becoming literate.'

'I know how to read,' Elwyn replied.

'Pardon?'

'I said, I know how to read.'

Timothy looked puzzled, but before he could say anything, there was a pounding at the front door, loud and determined enough to be heard down the hall. They waited for someone else to answer, but the knocking didn't stop.

'Piety? Boaz? Can one of you get the door? We are discussing our lesson plans,' Timothy shouted – shouting across rooms was forbidden in the Blackwell house, but this didn't seem to bother Timothy when it came to his own behaviour. 'We have this time scheduled. We mustn't be bothered.' There was no answer. 'Of course, she had to choose this afternoon to go for one of her long walks. . .' Timothy muttered to himself. 'Excuse me one moment, Nephew.' He got up and left the room, then a few minutes later an angry voice filled the hall. Elwyn went to see what the fuss was about, and once he was in view of the front door, a slender, red-faced man pointed furiously at him.

'That's him! That's the forest trash that stole Miss Rhoad's goat!'

The man pushed past Timothy and lunged sloppily at Elwyn. Elwyn had spent his life hunting; his reflexes were sharp. He dodged, and the man tripped on the carpet, landing face first on the floor.

# CHAPTER 6

# The Goat Girl

Elwyn bent down over the man.

'Oh dear. I think he's dead.' Timothy pulled at his beard anxiously. 'I did nothing to provoke him. He was out of his mind.'

'He's not dead,' Elwyn said. 'He smells like he's been drinking. He hit his head on the floor.'

Timothy adjusted his glasses.

'Help me move him to the couch,' Elwyn said. They heaved the body over, bumping into several pieces of furniture, Timothy nearly dropping his side more than once. The man's shoes were caked with mud. 'Who is he?' Elwyn asked.

'Said he worked in the stables of Cronus Rhoad, but I can hardly believe that. Rhoad's running for the Chancellorship. He would be more careful who he hires.'

'Why is he here?'

'Just like you said. Drunk. And in the middle of the day, too. He was raving about some goat he's boarding that belongs to Rhoad's daughter.'

'Goat?' Elwyn felt light-headed again.

'Why Rhoad's daughter would have a goat is beyond me. Unruly animals.'

Elwyn walked back out the still-open door, where the air smelt of grass and the sun shone on the stone street. He shaded his eyes to try and catch a glimpse of the animal that had followed him on his walk from the station, but he saw nothing. So he went back inside, and got the slightly chewed shirt he was wearing when he arrived. He threw it out the door and watched.

'What are you doing?' Timothy said. Elwyn put a finger to his lips, but kept his eyes on the shirt on the stone path. Sure enough, after a minute or two the animal came cautiously over and began to chew on what was left of the buttons. Elwyn grabbed the goat around its shoulders and used the shirt as a makeshift collar.

His uncle came out of the house, squinting in the sunlight and looking up and down the street.

'Where does this Rhoad live?' Elwyn asked.

'Down the road a mile or two. . . the big place, over the river. But, Elwyn, our lesson time is of utmost importance. We have a schedule to adhere to,' Timothy said, his pink face turning back towards the house. 'This man is clearly unbalanced. I don't see any reason to believe this is actually Miss Rhoad's goat.'

'I'm not going to let anyone think I'm a thief,' Elwyn said. Timothy hesitated, flustered. 'Over the river?'

'Yes,' Timothy consented. 'To the north, impossible to miss. It's his summer residence, gaudy as anything, even for a businessman and aspiring politician.'

'I'll be back soon. If the man wakes up, let him know

where I've gone.' Elwyn started leading the goat north. He was hungry and annoyed about the accusation of goat-stealing, but he couldn't resist giving the animal a scratch between the horns. The sun was hot and breezeless, and Elwyn walked as quickly as he could. On the streets, people again stared. A child walking with his mother pointed at Elwyn and began to say something before she hushed him and rushed away. 'This is all your fault, you know,' Elwyn said to the goat as it reached its neck out to try to get a bite of Elwyn's trousers.

The Rhoad house was as easy to find as Timothy said it would be. It was a great, gleaming place, built on top of a hill instead of under it. It sat like a crown on the north side of the river, massive white walls studded with windows. The front door had swirling decorative glass set into the wood, and there was a button beside it with the words PUSH HERE on a brass plate. When Elwyn pushed, he could hear a ringing inside the house – not just an ordinary bell, but several of them, playing out a tune.

Elwyn was surprised when the woman who opened the door was very old and frowning. He expected the inhabitants of the house to be as glamorous as its exterior. She stood before Elwyn, a chandelier twinkling from the ceiling behind her.

'Hello,' Elwyn said. 'You must be Mrs Rhoad. I've come to return your daughter's goat.'

The woman cackled, exposing a large gap where teeth were missing. 'Mrs Rhoad! I haven't heard that one before.'

Behind her, Elwyn could hear music playing. The woman was still laughing, but Elwyn's gaze went from her into the hall beyond, where he could see large vases of hothouse flowers and gilded frames. It was a glimpse, only a glimpse. But Elwyn felt immediately bound to the house, whether by desire or destiny, he didn't know. He wanted to see more, wanted it desperately. He had this feeling that his future was somewhere in those halls. The goat strained on its makeshift collar, trying to get inside.

'You know, I'm really thirsty from the walk over.'

The old woman laughed again, but there was a bit of malice in her voice. 'I bet you are. Want to come inside, don't you? I've seen little Forester thieves like you before.'

'I'm not a thief, I'm trying to do the right thing. I. . .' Elwyn began. 'Is this your goat or not?' He unwrapped his shirt from around the animal, ostensibly to give the woman a better look. But as he did, the goat ran around her legs into the house. The woman went into panic about the floors.

Elwyn didn't hide his smile as he went in, trying to help the woman chase down the animal. All houses are their own small worlds, contained and complete, and Elwyn got to see inside a new one as he scrambled after the goat. He saw gleaming brass phonograph horns, massive paintings, and everywhere, glass, glass, glass. Perfect, clear glass bringing light in.

The creature was loud on the tile floors, and down a hallway, a door opened. Out stepped a red-headed girl about Elwyn's own age, and at the sight of her, Elwyn tripped over the animal, who had turned and rushed towards the girl.

Elwyn scrambled to get up off the ground, but the girl wasn't paying attention to him. Her arms were around the trouble-making goat, looking into its eyes and hugging him to her. In her presence, Elwyn found himself unable to move; it was like a new wind was inside him, shaking down the leaves from every tree, troubling all still waters.

Then, a pair of lean legs blocked his view. Elwyn rose to his feet. The man Elwyn faced was half a head taller than he was and much older, in his fifties at least. The age could only be seen in the thin lines on the man's face, tiny wrinkles in his neck, faint spots on his hands. He didn't hold himself like a middle-aged man, or have that 'good steadying-weight,' as Badfishians called the customary thickening that followed settling down, having children. He looked well-composed, self-assured. 'What are you doing here?' he said, his voice clear and firm.

'I'm Elwyn. I came to Liberty to live with my aunt Piety Blackwell and her husband Timothy Blackwell. I came to study. To make something of myself,' Elwyn said, trying to use the man's clear tone.

'No,' the man said. 'I mean, what are you doing in my *house*?'

The woman who had been at the front door finally caught up to them.

'I'll check his pockets, Mr Rhoad,' she said, her arms reaching out for Elwyn like knotty branches.

Rhoad raised his hand. 'That won't be necessary, Nan.'

'Look! He brought Willoughby,' the red-headed girl said, only looking away from the goat for a moment. Her eyes lit on Elwyn and didn't look displeased. She returned to the goat, beaming. 'I missed you!' she said as she rubbed Willoughby under the chin.

'Get that creature out of here,' the old woman said, shooing the goat with her apron, to no effect. Elwyn's gaze was again locked on that smiling girl. But the man placed a coin in Elwyn's palm.

'Thank you for delivering my daughter's goat. Your help will no longer be needed,' he said with a nod to the old woman. She guided Elwyn out of the house, muttering under her breath about Forester thieves coming up from the fields and causing trouble.

As soon as Elwyn was on the front steps, the door shut firmly behind him. But he returned to his uncle's house feeling light, stopping to pat a few horses on the nose and look in a few shop windows. Elwyn arrived late for dinner. Between bites from a large slice of Mirth's cake, Timothy delivered a lecture on dedication, responsibility, sacrifice and, again, punctuality. Elwyn was sent to his room. His stomach ached at the sight of that cake, but he didn't complain. He went to his room as he was told. There in the quiet and growing shadows, he sat down on his bed to inspect the missing buttons from his shirt to see what needed to be mended.

The bedframe below him groaned for a moment, then collapsed altogether onto the ground. And as it did, it pulled on a small string that was attached to the headboard and ran previously unnoticed up the wall to the shining wooden ceiling fan. The fan turned on, flinging from its blades bits of mud and leaves all over the room, onto the fresh bed and Elwyn's new clothes.

Elwyn had never seen a ceiling fan before. At first he wondered if it was malfunctioning. But then he heard laughter from the bedroom door. Boaz smirked, looking even more pinched than before. But Elwyn liked pranks and mischief of all kinds, and he knew that appearances could be deceiving – wise old owls were the most foolish birds in the forest; flippant-looking jay birds were real sages. As more dirt assailed him, he smiled at his cousin.

'Pretty good set-up,' Elwyn said.

The boy stopped laughing. And Elwyn could see, through the dirt clinging to his eyelashes, that there wasn't anything jolly in his cousin's face.

'This is my house, forest trash,' Boaz said, standing still as the fan's breeze tossed the loose leaves. 'You are not welcome here.'

# CHAPTER 7

# *Sparks*

WHEN THE FIRST elderflowers bloomed, Whim Moone picked two large clumps and put them in a vase on the kitchen table. Her father came home and saw the flowers and smiled. Together they dipped them in batter and fried them and ate them hot. Elderflower season was brief, and the rest of it would be spent foraging and distilling liquor from the blossoms. Every year Whim drank one small cup. It was sweet.

The first letter came from Elwyn that same day. Whim went down to the post office, where March Wilder was behind the counter sorting mail. There was a stack of newspapers for Whim's father and a few invoices for the Moone's distillery. The letter from Liberty was in the middle of it all, its heavy paper crisp and white against cheap newsprint.

Whim opened it right away. She read about Elwyn's long days in his uncle's office, the memorised facts, the prank his cousin played on him and the hour Elwyn spent cleaning the bits of leaves from the wool bedspread. But that wasn't the majority of the letter. Elwyn went on and on about a house he had visited, a house on a hill. It had been full of light, beautiful things, beautiful people.

> *I don't know how to describe it to you, Whim. You know how the woods look in May? When the leaves are new and the sun comes through them fresh and clean like water comes up from a spring? That's how it felt inside that house. The world didn't seem like an old place, stuck in the past. It seemed like a place anything could happen. I felt my future there, Whim. I just wish you could have been there to see it with me.*

'Letter from the Bramble boy?' March asked as Whim read it again. Reading Elwyn's thoughts, seeing his handwriting made her feel the distance between them very keenly. But she couldn't stop reading. She was greedy for his words, even as they gave her an ache in her belly. 'That's the wonderful thing about working in a post office,' March went on. 'Some people think it's a frivolous job, but it's the most important work in the world. You're a strand in a web that connects people.'

Whim smiled. She kept the folded letter in the pocket by her chest as she carried her father's mail back to their house down low on the banks by the marshes.

Whim didn't have time to write back to Elwyn right away. There was a lot work to be done in the early summer season, when the leaves and shoots were young. The Moones came from a long line of herbalists, brewers, steepers, apothecaries, distillers. Most male Badfishians spent their springs planting Hill crops and their late summers harvesting them, but not Whim's father, nor his father before him nor his grandfather nor great-grandfather. While some people had been driven to sell their labour to pay their taxes and buy their tools, the Moones still made their own way.

Whim put the letters against the vase on the kitchen table and picked up her basket, which she carried through the woods to fill with flowers. The sun had finished drying the dew even in the shade and the wind was growing hot. Whim worked quickly, filling her baskets with early elder-flower blossoms from the patch down by the old south road, but as she worked, over the forest sounds of the birds and squirrels and the snip of her shears, there was a noise that was rare in their part of the world: the grumble of an engine, the crunching of wheels against stone. Whim looked up at the dirt road beyond her.

She had seen cars before. Once or twice a year, one would pass through on its way to no-one-knew-where. But this was different. These trucks were large and long, yellow as the petals of a black-eyed-susan. The neglected road groaned with their weight. She counted as they passed. There were four.

By lunchtime the morning chores were finished. Her father left the distillery and entered the house, wiping the midday heat from his face. Whim had set the table for them – a vase with a branch of elder, two linen napkins, two plates. She poached them each a goose egg, which they ate with pearly cattail roots and lettuce.

Aelred Moon was quiet at the table, cutting into his egg with a fork. His eyes were handsome even when he was dark or sad, but that day he smiled and Whim smiled back at him, finally feeling something like herself again.

'I saw something interesting today,' Whim said, taking a drink of chilled birch tea. A knob of ice from their ice house clanked against the glass.

'And what was that, little Whim?'

'Automobiles. Four of them. They were there on the south road.'

She took a bite of lettuce, expecting interest. But instead a wrinkle formed between Aelred's eyes.

'I've never seen anything like it. They were big and long, more like train cars than automobiles,' Whim continued.

She looked up from her plate at her father. Any laughter in his face had gone. He wiped his mouth with a napkin.

'Which way were they headed?'

'East.'

The wrinkle between his eyes had deepened. He seemed lost in thought.

'Is something wrong?' Whim asked.

Aelred shook his head as though shaking away flies. 'It's nothing.' He picked up his fork and ate a cattail root. He gave Whim a reassuring smile that seemed difficult for him.

They finished their lunch, both of them putting the incident behind them. Whim looked over the accounting log while her father cleared the dishes and swept the floor. When the day's heat had passed, they continued their work into evening – Whim in the forest, Aelred at the distillery. As the sun grew low, laughter and the smell of cooking fires began to perfume the settlement. Whim wrote at the little desk by her bedroom window, telling Elwyn the odds and ends that might interest him, and then she joined the others making their way up into the middle of town. The day's work was done. Old men shelled peas and told hunting stories, old women smoked pipes, and children poked embers with large sticks.

When the first squirrels were pulled from the fire, Caradoc Alfin began to play his concertina and Aelred joined in singing. The sun slanted through the trees, catching the leaves, and it looked like thousands of green lanterns in the branches. The meat was good. And the music was, too. Those summer nights had a way of seeing people past the small tensions and misgivings always present in tight-knit communities. A man swept up his wife and danced around and around the fire, and people began to clap along. Their faces were pink with pleasure. Whim smiled as she walked towards the Bramble house. Mirth was outside the open front door, talking to the mother of Allun's fiancée and eyeing the roast squirrel.

The Bramble house was an old place, one of the few still built around the trunk of a tree, and it was nearly as familiar to Whim as her own. She had lived there for a year after her mother died. Her father had been unwell, and Mirth had feared the effect of it all on the young, quiet girl. In her forceful, forthright way – still regarded with some suspicion – Mirth insisted on taking little Whim until Aelred sobered up and was able to care for a child. In time he was grateful. But he still felt an uneasiness around Mirth, that Hill woman marrying into the Forester ways, tough and pushy as an ox. Whim didn't feel that way. To her, Mirth was strong and natural as the trees themselves.

Whim said hello to her before she climbed up the branch of the low oak, where Enid and Neste Bramble dangled their legs and shared a bowl of pickled fiddleheads. Enid was telling a story about tracking a fox. She had finally found its den and was waiting in a tree for it to emerge when she saw Elis Arwell passing by on the lake path some thirty yards away. He was shirtless with a fishing pole over his shoulder, and she stood up and leant around the trunk to get a better look. She leant and leant and leant so far, she fell right out of the tree, flat on the ground, just as the fox was poking its nose from its hole.

'All in all, worth it for a better look at Elis in just his undershorts,' Enid said. Whim was laughing and took a fiddlehead as Neste, never liking to be outdone, began her own story.

As they talked, the sun sank below the horizon. Sparks flew up and faded. Aelred had gathered a crowd of children around him, telling the story, as he had done many times before, of the beginning of the Collective:

'In the beginning, there was the sky and there was water. And in time, land pushed its way up, and creatures crawled onto this land, and we people lived in the middle of it all. But there was just one big slice of land on that giant water, and life got a bit boring for everyone. So to keep things interesting, the land broke up into hundreds of pieces. All different sizes: some cold, some warm, some flat, some tall, some bare, some full of mountains and rivers. And the creatures, now a good distance away from each other, found their own ways of being, of looking, of talking to each other.

'But we people thought we were clever. We made boats and used them to trade ideas and goods. And then, when we got tired of that, we turned each other into ideas and goods. Sold each other. Killed each other for a bit more land. Worked each other to death for a bit more money.

'But it didn't go on like that for ever. Those who were oppressed rose up against their oppressors. The factories were burnt down, the slave-owners killed; war broke out. Justice, you see, doesn't come easy. The war was long and terrible, and the land we love was soaked in blood. By the time it was over, we hardly knew who we were any more, or who anyone else had been.

'Then, from the ashes of what had been our cities rose new ideas. Some people, like the Hill folks, wanted to return to the farms and rebuild the cities, but this time more gently, more removed from foreign greed and ideas. Not us. We Foresters didn't want to be a part of any kind of domination. We returned to the land to live in harmony with it, not to rule over it. And so for these 180 years, we've lived a life of peace, with our place and, what is even more difficult, with the other people who inhabit it.'

That was where the story ended. The children didn't stay up much longer than that. Drinks were poured and the music grew slower. Dewey, the second-oldest of the Bramble kids, shook the branch to tease Whim, and then sat down beside his sisters and ate the rest of the fiddleheads.

As Whim sat in the tree, the talk and world growing quiet around her, the thought of taking Elwyn up on his offer, joining him in Liberty, passed through her mind. It did every night. But that evening as the darkness grew deeper, as fathers carried the last children to bed, most of them already asleep on warm shoulders, she felt no regret. None. It was just a typical summer night in Badfish Creek, but Whim did not take it for granted. That evening under the stars, she felt keenly the value of what she had, and she held it very close and very dear.

Aelred did not need to ask his daughter about the automobiles again. The next day they came back, not just driving by, but parking right in the middle of Badfish Creek. The paths were only just wide enough and branches broke and groaned as the trucks parked.

'Don't mind us. We are just here to collect some data and take some measurements,' the men said, stepping out of their vehicles.

# CHAPTER 8

# Stirring

WHIM GATHERED FLOWERING MINT that grew along the east side of the house. She put the herbs and water in a large glass jar and set it along the south-side wall to steep until the water was dark and the sun-tea could be strained. Whim had meant to set out the tea first thing in the morning, but she woke to an empty house; when she went down to the distillery to see if her father was there, she found the stills untended and herbs still heaped in their baskets.

It was Sunday, but the work had to be done. She started a batch of medicines before the plants lost their potency, prepared a shipment of liquors, balanced the accounting book. She went back home, washed, ate her egg. Put out the tea. Still, her father was not home. Whim spread a napkin on the kitchen table. On it she set a boiled duck egg, a jar of cold watercress soup and a wooden spoon. Her hands moved with ease as she folded and tied the napkin sides, but she didn't feel the same ease inside. She carried the bundle out into the woods.

It was not a long walk to the road, but it was enough to get a sense of the forest. Everything was quiet, but also almost electric. She could sense the buzz of the leaves as they fanned out for the sun's rays. It was a perfect noon, full of the life that was usually invigorating, but that day it agitated her.

Coming over a hill, beyond the elder and sassafras, Whim saw her father. He was in the same place he had spent so much of the last couple weeks, a few feet from the road, sitting with his back against a tree. Every day since the trucks left Badfish Creek with samples and charts, Aelred had been spending more and more time there. He sat with a notebook in hand, recording any automobiles. When he wasn't there by the road, he wasn't at the distillery or in the kitchen. He was at his desk, sending letters or reading and mailing articles to underground newspapers.

When Whim reached him, Aelred looked up at his daughter and smiled. But his face was worn. Little grey hairs had formed around his temples. She crouched down and spread out the napkin.

'You forgot to eat breakfast again,' she said.

'Whim, you are a treasure and a delight for ever.'

The road was silent, and he looked away from it while he ate with his daughter. For a moment, he was himself again.

'So, little apple blossom. What fine plans do you have this Sabbath day?'

Whim lay on the ground, her stomach on the cool earth. Ants crawled in front of her on their urgent, mysterious paths.

'I'll pay a luncheon visit, then I think I'll go home and paint.'

'A day fit for a queen!'

Whim didn't ask how he would be spending his Sunday. He would be there by the road. Recording. Waiting. She was quiet, and her face must have betrayed some of her feelings.

'What is it, my Whim?'

She looked up at her father, but she didn't know how to say the things that were troubling her. Whim tried to smile for him as she excused herself. Then she walked back home and prepared for lunch. With a basket of cakes and a couple of jars of dandelion-blossom jam, yellow as summer, she set off to the Brambles'. Outside the shelter of her shady stone home, the air had grown hot. But it was still the early days of summer; Badfishians hadn't yet got into the habit of closing up the house after breakfast to keep out the swampy heat. Children wandered in and out of doors; people called out of windows, sweat misting on their skin.

Whim hooked the basket under her arm as she arrived at the Brambles' home. Mirth was at the sink washing dishes while Neste and Enid played keep-away with Loew's Sunday hat. They laughed as the hat flew back and forth across the room. Mirth turned around and saw the game. Her eyes widened.

'Enid! Neste!' They handed the hat back to Loew, and Enid mussed his hair. He ran off. 'Sunday visitors might arrive any moment,' Mirth said. 'If you have so much time, you can help me tidy up. Oh, Whim,' she said, noticing her at last. 'Hello, dear.' She came over and gave her an absent-minded kiss on the cheek. 'I'll have the table set soon. Enid, Neste, go brush your hair again. You look like a pair of ragamuffins.'

'Come with us, Whim,' Neste said, always unruffled. The girls' room was up the ladder. Its wooden walls were decorated in clippings from newspapers: singers and actors they had heard at the phonograph parlour in Kegonsa that they saved their money to attend. The parlour was a tiny place, a dry-goods store during the day. The sisters were absolute experts on these phonographs, insofar as they could be.

Enid sat on the bed while Neste looked at her hair in the battered mirror and took her comb from its case. It was bone and had been her grandmother's, given to her on her sixteenth birthday. Enid – two years her junior with Elwyn in between – said it would have been awful to be the second daughter if she had been unlucky enough to have any interest in things like combs.

'Have you heard from our brother lately?' Neste asked pleasantly. 'He hasn't written to us.'

'Horrible brother. I'd hate him if I didn't miss him,' Enid said.

'I hear from him,' Whim said, looking out the window at the leafy world.

'What does he say?' Neste asked, fixing her hair in a complicated bun. 'Enid, how does this look?'

'Like a deer's ass,' Enid replied.

'I don't think he's gotten much of a welcome. Your cousin sounds especially unkind, though Elwyn doesn't say it outright. You know Elwyn – he always tries to make things sound bright,' she said. 'Your uncle pays Elwyn a lot of attention, but it sounds like it's mostly focused on a book he's writing. He has Elwyn on a very strict schedule – a lot of memorisation, a lot of studying, a lot of rules.'

'Well, that's what he gets for leaving us and acting so high and mighty,' Enid said.

'And he keeps writing about his first day there, how through all these strange circumstances he wound up visiting a big house on a hill. He said it was like something out of a dream. . .'

'Oh, I'm tired of hearing about Elwyn's dreams,' Enid said.

Whim sighed. 'Me too.'

Neste looked at Whim from the mirror.

'Are you all right?' Neste asked.

'She's still upset with Elwyn for leaving us. We all are,' Enid said. 'Don't worry,' she said, turning to Whim. 'The second you two are old enough, he'll be back and you'll run off and get married. We all know it.'

Whim's cheeks flushed.

'Enid,' Neste said. 'Leave them alone.'

'It's a good thing, too,' Enid went on. 'You are one of the few girls we could tolerate our brother marrying. Not like that awful Posy who weaselled her way in with Allun.'

'Mam will hear you.'

'Let her hear.'

'It's nothing to do with Elwyn leaving. It's about my father,' Whim said, suddenly flushing. 'Elwyn says not to trouble myself over those trucks. He said my father is "wonderful, but also mistrustful and sort of intense". He thinks it will pass.' Whim swallowed. Enid and Neste were for once silent, listening. 'Elwyn's probably right,' she went on. 'But he's not here. He doesn't have to see what I see every morning. My father doesn't sleep any more. He doesn't go to the distillery. Liberty seems further away every day. . .'

Mirth yelled for them to come down to eat. Whim was relieved not to have to finish explaining herself. On their way to the table, Neste put a hand on Whim's shoulder.

'It will pass,' she said.

The Brambles' table was a big round one that had belonged to Elwyn's paternal great-grandmother. It was decorated with table linens that Mirth had brought with her when she married, and loaded with acorn bread, a pile of cured meats, wild berries and strong dandelion coffee. It was a lot of food for not many people – Allun was visiting his fiancée's family, and Dewey, Teilo and Teilo's chicken had tagged along with him; Posy had two pretty younger sisters, one with a tame sparrow.

Old Finchy filled one of the empty places. She didn't spend much time outside her house any more, except to sit on a little bench with her lace and bobbins and a long tobacco pipe. Her skin was weather-worn and leathery, but though she was very old, the oldest woman in Badfish Creek, her hair never greyed. It was still thick and dark, pulled into a large knot that looked too heavy for her head.

Finchy inspected the plates while everyone else ate. She took a pollen cake, smelt it, then took a bird-sized bite and chewed slowly. She made a face of displeasure and swallowed a gulp of coffee before taking another tiny peck.

'Is it true what they are saying about Aelred?' Loew asked into the silence that had come over the girls as they enthusiastically ate.

'Shh,' Neste said gently.

Loew went on, 'I heard he thinks the world is going to end.'

'Quiet, Loew. Mr Moone doesn't think the world is going to end,' Mirth said and looked cautiously up at Finchy, whose small nearsighted eyes were fixed ahead as usual.

Whim looked over at curious Loew, everyone's favourite Bramble kid. She took a sip of her dandelion coffee for a bit of courage. 'He doesn't think the world is going to end. He just thinks that *our* world is going to end,' she said. 'That is, if we don't do anything to protect it.'

Loew's face screwed up. 'What do you mean?' he asked through a bite of bread.

'Watch your manners,' Mirth scolded.

'If the world is going to end, life will end for all people everywhere,' Whim said. 'Every community in all four territories will be gone. The Collective will end. The whole world. That's not what my father's worried about.'

'What's he worried about, then?' Enid asked.

'There are rumours that some small towns like ours have been broken up. And the land has been taken,' Whim said, a slight tremble in her voice. The words she had heard so often from her father sounded strange in her own mouth. 'There was a river town in the south like ours. They say that there were a lot of trucks seen in that part of the country, and then the people were told they had to leave.'

Loew, Neste and Enid were listening attentively now. Mirth was watching Finchy, and Finchy looked down at her plate as though she was falling asleep.

'My father is afraid the same thing is going to happen here, happen in all the forest homesteads.' She paused. 'He has been keeping track of the comings and goings of any trucks, keeping in close contact with some underground newspapers for word from other communities. He doesn't want anyone to catch us off-guard.'

Finchy's face was still looking down at her plate, her shoulders bent, when she spoke. 'Your father is a trouble-maker,' she said. When she looked up, her tiny eyes were dark.

'What?' Whim said.

'My great-great-grandmother was one of the founders of Badfish Creek after the Second War. She carried three children through the woods to this place, and my great-great-grandfather pulled the wagon. The Second War – do you even know what war means, girl? Blood. Blood was spilt for this land. It was earned.' Finchy's chin was trembling. 'I've lived a long time. And the only trouble I've ever seen hasn't been from people out there. It's been from fools like your father stirring people up.' Finchy's face began to look younger, ire bringing colour to her dark, worn cheeks. People like your father aren't happy unless they are making fools of themselves and everyone around them.'

Whim felt her face reddening. 'Take it back,' she said with a firmness that surprised her.

Finchy smiled toothlessly. 'Your father is a fool, and he is making trouble for us all.'

'Mam, can I go to my room?' Loew asked. Mirth nodded, her eyes quickly returning to the scene at the table. Her body was tense.

'My father loves Badfish Creek. He wouldn't do any-thing—' Whim began.

'He is always up to something. Schemes. Conspiracies. He and his ideas are not welcome here, I can tell you that.' There was a look of disgust on Old Finchy's face, a look that seared Whim.

'Who are you to judge what does and doesn't belong here? You who sit in your big old house and make lace you never sell or give to anyone. You just put it up in your windows and go out on Sundays to eat at other people's tables without ever inviting anyone to your own. I don't have to listen to who you think is of use or isn't,' Whim said, face flushed and words pouring from her. She looked around the table at the astonished faces. 'Excuse me, Mirth,' Whim said and she left the house.

'Whim—' Mirth called after her, but Whim didn't turn. Her eyes burned with angry tears. Her walk turned into a run, tears flowing freely now. Finchy was touchy and difficult, not someone whose opinion Whim held in high regard. But seeds of doubt had been growing in Whim's mind. Though she had spent her life admiring her father, it didn't make much sense. Why, again, was it such a bad sign to see a few automobiles? Why would they trust second-hand news about a distant homestead in the south?

Like she often did when something was too much to bear, Whim left town to walk along the marshes and low hills. The afternoon heat was oppressive; by the time she returned home, beads of sweat were rolling down the back of her neck. The house felt cool and pleasantly dark and quiet. She retreated to her room and shut the door behind her. Her space was decorated with fabric and polished stones. An easel stood in the corner. She picked up her paints. The sun came in low through the window, alighting on a tiny glass prism that sent hundreds of little dancing white lights around the room.

She was finishing the purple-white of a cloud when she heard a knock on the door.

'Come in,' she said.

Her father stepped into the room and stood behind her for a while, watching the brushstrokes and paint on canvas.

'You always remind me of your mother when you paint,' he said.

'It makes me think of her,' Whim said.

'I'm sorry I haven't been here, Whim.'

She put down her paintbrush and turned to look at her father. He looked worn, but there was kindness in his tired eyes and drooping limbs.

'Even when I have been here, I haven't been here,' he said. 'And I'm sorry. I won't do that again.'

'Did they tell you?'

He put a hand on his daughter's head.

'She's an old woman, Whim. Let her think what she will think. Let her talk. What I worry about is my own soul. And it won't let me rest if I do you wrong. And me neglecting you and my work? That's doing you wrong.'

Whim stood and threw her arms around her father. She didn't often show affection so strongly or abruptly, but she did then. The world felt right for the first time in what seemed like so long.

'Father?' Whim asked, returning to her chair and holding the paintbrush in her fingers.

'Yes, little Whim?'

'Do you really think that our world is going to end?'

Aelred knelt down beside his daughter and looked at her directly.

'I don't know. But whatever is in store for us, from now on, we will face it together.'

Her father stood and walked out of her room of dancing light.

'Did you eat dinner?' he remembered, turning around in the doorway.

'I wasn't hungry.'

'Can I bring you something?'

'I'll come out. We'll eat together.'

Whim cleaned her paintbrushes, and Aelred prepared the dumplings. And as the sun set, they ate a large dinner with the doors and windows open to the sounds of other meals and laughter, and the sounds of frogs and crickets; and the lights of the fireflies beginning to blink on and off.

The next day, the relocation notices arrived.

# CHAPTER 9

# *Hunger*

After two weeks at the Blackwells', Elwyn found he was hungry. The hunger was like a fire inside him. He was hungry when he woke. He was hungry when he sat down to breakfast. He was hungry when the maid cleared the plates, and he and Timothy sat down in the library – Timothy's library – and worked through hours of books, tests, exercises.

'Your future lies before you, an improved self, a civilised life. One musn't be distracted by anything,' Timothy said and wrote '*Trouble concentrating*' in his notes. Elwyn tried to ignore the feeling, but it kept burning in him. And also burning in him, distracting him from the work at the desk, were Elwyn's memories of the Rhoad house. He had only been there a few minutes, but every detail cast a vivid impression: the light through the glass, the light on the girl's hair, the light off the vases. The images danced in his mind, growing and growing. Every day Elwyn worked with Timothy, glimmers of that place would appear like the sun reflecting off the chandelier. It made an ache in his chest like the ache in his stomach.

Elwyn didn't bear it entirely quietly. Between work-books and recitations, he'd ask his uncle questions: *Who is Rhoad? Where did he come from? What is his daughter like?* Timothy mistook these questions for an interest in civics, and answered them gladly. He told Elwyn that the house he had seen was the Rhoads' summer residence. The rest of the year they spent at an equally gaudy house in St Louis, where Rhoad ran his business and, now, his political campaign. After making a fortune in lead mines, Rhoad was entering public service, campaigning for the Chancellorship of the Central Homesteads, campaigning with Mrs Rhoad, who was his third wife, and their daughter Hestia, who was a year older than Elwyn.

Timothy also loaned Elwyn a book on the lives of prominent businessmen in America. It had a section on Rhoad, but Timothy encouraged his nephew to look at the stories of less garish examples – there were plenty of people who made their fortunes more slowly, deliberately, traditionally. But it was Rhoad's story that Elwyn read again and again. Rhoad, like Elwyn, came from poverty: his father had worked on riverboats, his mother had died young. Rhoad ran away when he was fourteen and began trading on the river. At sixteen, he drove lumber down the Messipi from the Northwoods to New Orleans, then walked the river north again and used the profit to buy part of a lumber mill, then lead mines, and on and on. There was colour to the stories: floods, fires, bandits, wife-wooing.

It was colour much needed on summer days that seemed long and dim. Study was constant, broken only by meals – and those meals were observed in silence. Occasionally Piety and Timothy talked business – menu plans, instructions for the housekeeper, clothes that needed pressing – but even this was done in reserved tones. Elwyn was used to a loud home: Enid and Dewey arguing, Teilo trying to bring his chicken to dinner, Neste's laugh, his mother's scolding. He never thought the noises would be the thing he missed most from home.

But the days went on. He studied. He didn't break the silence at dinner. He didn't return his cousin's glares. He didn't complain about the hunger in his stomach, in his heart. He followed all the rules.

Then one night, Elwyn's stomach woke him and wouldn't let him back asleep. He stared up at the stars through the skylight, then finally got out of bed and walked the dark halls to the pantry, which was beautifully stocked with rows and rows of jams and dried meats, cheeses and breads – all forbidden between meals. Elwyn grabbed what he could and began slicing away in the empty kitchen, tossing piece after piece into his mouth, hungrier and hungrier with each bite. He was so busy with this slicing and eating, he didn't hear anyone enter the kitchen until he heard the kettle clank on the stove.

Elwyn jumped. Aunt Piety faced him, chin high, arms folded. His mother had the same way of standing when Elwyn was in trouble – like when he once followed a passing caravan going downstream and returned two days later with his skin scraped and his clothes ruined. Mirth was more formidable than her sister: taller, wider, like a bear. But Elwyn was used to his mother. Her anger often made him laugh. His aunt was a stranger. He froze for a minute. Then, thinking, he turned back to the food and kept slicing.

'Can I get you some?' he said. 'This cheese is good with the jam, I think.'

He felt his aunt staring as he found another plate and made a large sandwich. He turned to her, holding out the food and trying to look friendly. The kettle was steaming, but she hadn't moved. Elwyn couldn't read her like he could read his mother. She stared at him, not taking the plate, not smiling. Then, without saying anything, she walked over to the pantry, took a jar down from the top shelf and held it out to Elwyn.

'Blackcurrant,' she said, 'is better with that cheese.' Her lips were tight, but there was a spark of humour in her eyes. She took the plate and poured the hot water into a teapot. 'Follow me,' she ordered, picking up the tea. The two of them took their sandwiches to Piety's parlour, which had lamps nicely arranged and lit, a plate of crackers. 'I'm fond of a midnight snack myself,' Piety said.

'Isn't it against the rules?'

'A person should take pleasure where they can find it.'

Elwyn smiled, though his aunt did not. The room was cool, and Elwyn relaxed into his chair. He felt comfortable for the first time in weeks. 'I see why you spend so much time here,' Elwyn said, looking around at the pictures on the walls, the plants in pots.

'There are many reasons I spend time here,' Piety said archly, pouring them both tea and blowing on hers.

'I've been wanting to thank you again,' Elwyn said, 'for letting me come here. For all your letters. They meant a lot to me growing up. Even when you stopped writing, I still read the old ones over and over. I kept them all. They made me believe in myself, believe I could be more than what I saw around me.'

Piety's mouth tightened into a sour smirk. She took a small sip of tea that was too hot and burnt. 'Do you know when I started writing to you?'

'When I was four.'

'I had come to your town. Taken the train, walked from the station. Your grandfather had died – your mother's father and mine. He had been a taciturn man, unkind to his animals and cold to his family. He disowned Mirth when she married a Forester, and I hadn't been in contact with him for years. For a while, I regretted that. I went to see him in his last days. I wanted to tell Mirth he was sick, but he held a grudge against her even on his deathbed. After he died, I went to tell your mother about his passing. I wasn't looking forward to it, and not just because I didn't want to be the bearer of bad news – I knew that for someone like her, not being invited to her father's funeral would be unforgivable. But I went anyway.'

Piety chuckled sardonically. 'The trip was worse than I imagined. Mirth's life had become so limited, and it was hard for me to see at a time when I felt so much was possible. But there, surrounded by kids playing in the dirt was you: a four-year-old boy in a largely illiterate community, reading a book.'

Elwyn enjoyed stories like this. He smiled. 'I like reading.'

'It reminded me of myself. I had been a young girl who loved learning who lived in a home where learning wasn't valued. I used books to claw my way out of the life I was born into. And back then, when I first saw you, I was proud of what I had done. I thought I had achieved something. I went to university. I married a wealthy, intelligent man. I had a child. But in time I would find that the world I had fought my way into was empty.'

The smile on Elwyn's face began to fade.

'Timothy wanted you to come here. He wanted to work on this project with you, help you move up in the world with the hope that it would help him. But I want you to know that I was against it, Elwyn.'

'I don't understand,' Elwyn said. The sandwich became sandy in his mouth, and it was hard to swallow.

The tea had cooled enough for Piety to take a larger sip. Her eyes again looked sharp above the rim of the cup. 'This,' she said, nodding to the room around her, 'is worth nothing. Don't waste your youth striving for a hollow prize.'

'I want more than this, too,' Elwyn said. He spoke almost urgently, wanting his aunt to understand. 'I want a house like Cronus Rhoad's, and life with adventure and travel—'

'You misunderstand me, Elwyn. It all is empty,' Piety said, setting her cup down in her saucer. And Elwyn tried to take another bite, but the bread stuck to the top of his mouth. 'You were better off where you were. Timothy wanted you here. I think we're all better off left alone.'

# CHAPTER 10

# *Rally!*

WHIM DIDN'T WRITE to Elwyn about the relocation notices. Nor that her father's suspicions had been confirmed. She wanted to believe that this was out of respect for Mirth, that Elwyn's mother should be the one to tell him the news. But in the chaos that followed the arrival of the notices, Whim hadn't spoken to Mirth, nor had she sought her out. She knew deep down that her silence towards Elwyn was less to do with his mother and more to do with the fact that she feared he'd be indifferent. Not indifferent to her, but what was much worse – indifferent to the things Whim believed were the most important: love of a place, a people.

Elwyn, though, continued to write. A week after the relocation notices, another letter arrived. It didn't mention Aunt Piety, her advice or Elwyn's frustrations; it wasn't his habit to dwell on things that were dark – at least not out loud. Instead the letter was much like the last, focusing on things Elwyn hoped for, as bright and insubstantial as the light he described in the Rhoad family's summer home. It wasn't until the end that he addressed Whim's concerns about her father:

*I hope things are better with your dad. I hope it's not too hard on you. And I hope that one of these days you change your mind and come join me here!*

Whim had a drawer where she kept Elwyn's letters, tenderly folded. But this one she tore in two, threw into the cooking fire, and watched for the seconds it took to burn.

Outside her kitchen window, Badfish Creek moved like a disturbed anthill. The notices had been written in a confusing legal language. They cited a law that gave county overseers the right to seize land if its use was proven to be a danger to the Collective. Only two parts of the notices were written clearly: the threat of a forcible removal for any people who remained and the modest sum of money promised for a hasty departure.

The sum was small even by Badfishian standards, but money was money. It was easy to see who was going to take it. Rugs were being aired, linens washed, utensils scoured before being packed. The sunny rocks and branches of trees were billowing with blankets, bedspreads and curtains that would be whipped and stretched rid of wrinkles before being folded into chests and carried onto carts.

Whim didn't resent these families – the Brambles among them. There was too much going on to bother with resentment; she and her father were working doubly hard to get things laid by in the distillery while at the same time preparing a protest. The days were hot and the tasks were many, but everything was done in collaboration. It had been an exhilarating week.

That night, as the bats swooped and the fireflies lingered over tall grasses across the creek, people came to the Moone kitchen like moths to candle glow. Most of the men who sold their labour in the Hill fields were still gone – late June was the time for weeding and hay-mowing – but the room still quickly filled, some people having travelled many miles to get there after hearing the news.

Old Finchy sat in the corner, a wreath of smoke over her head. Her mouth was pursed tightly around the pipe's lip. Whim set out cups and a kettle of tea while she watched the old woman. The sight of Finchy there concerned Whim. She wondered when Finchy would break her silence and start scolding them all, calling them troublemakers. Not that it really mattered. What mattered was that her father had been right. Whim wouldn't doubt him again. Or herself.

She took a seat. People weren't talking much, which was unusual. They filled their cups and stood or sat and turned to look at Aelred, who was at the front of the room, raising his hands for attention.

'I'm glad you all have come. Tomorrow is the day. The day we rally. The day we face the men who stand against us,' Aelred said. As he spoke, a hush settled over the room. The oil lamp and candle shadows played on his face, and the fire reflected in his eyes. 'We'll cloak ourselves in red, march through Liberty to the town hall, and demand to know where the money is coming from, who is behind this. We will make our rights known.'

'Some of us have weapons, Aelred. We'll bring everything we have.' A voice from a darker side of the room spoke. It was Elwyn's brother Dewey, hands in fists.

'None of us will be armed. If we are seen as violent, they will have every excuse to use violence against us. If it's brute force against brute force, we will lose.'

'And you, Dewey Bramble, will be bringing nothing at all. You are too young to go.' The large figure of Mirth Bramble stepped through the open door, wiping her shoes aggressively on the rug before she entered. 'Aelred, what do you think you are doing? There are children here, and you're asking them to risk their necks for your ideas.'

'Not for my ideas. For our home, Mirth,' Aelred countered.

'Home or no home, we have to protect our children.'

'We have to protect our home *for* our children. The same thing happened in the town in the south. Some people left. Those that stayed behind were forced off. And when the land was empty, the houses flattened, what do you think they did? Within weeks, the earth had been hacked into mines.'

'I'm not an idiot, Aelred. I've read your pamphlets. But I've read other things, too. I've read accounts of the Second War. Children as young as twelve brought onto the battlefields. Fighting for causes that adults invented.

That's why those under twenty aren't allowed in militias any more, aren't allowed in battles. There were fields covered with young bodies, Aelred.'

'This is a protest, Mirth. It isn't a battle.'

'It isn't *their* battle,' she said.

Whim waited for her father to respond, but Aelred was quiet, looking at Mirth who stood immovably on the other side of the room.

'It doesn't matter what it is,' Dewey said. 'I turned twenty last week.'

'I know your age well enough, Dewey,' Mirth said. 'I've known you longer than you have known yourself. And I know you are hot-tempered and not at all ready for the things you think you are.'

'You don't know what I am ready for,' Dewey said.

'Oh, yes I do.'

Aelred raised his hand and the argument stopped, if just for a moment. Mirth's eyes were still on Dewey, challenging him to speak again.

'What goes on in your own household, Mirth, I will leave to you. But you are right. We would be fools not to learn from our past. I can promise that no one under twenty will be coming with us.'

There was a small murmur in the crowd, but few of the people there were young enough to be affected. It was Whim who felt this announcement deeply. She made a sound like she had been punctured. All the air left her.

'What do you mean?' she asked.

'We'll talk later, little Whim,' he said gently. But the rest of the night, while logistics were laid out, disguises were planned and old songs were sung, Whim's mind was stuck. Since the relocation notices had come, Whim and her father had been step-in-step, handing out flyers, sending word out to nearby communities. Despite the tragedy of it, the pain at the thought of losing everything, something had been kindled in her.

Finchy didn't speak. She had fallen asleep in her chair, and Whim had to wake her when the meeting was over. Finchy slapped her instinctively, like she always did when someone woke her. 'Good, peppery reflexes' is what she called it. 'Troublesome girl,' Finchy muttered on her way out, not apologising. People left slowly. The candles had burned low. The honeyed smell of wax permeated the small stone house, mixed with the smell of smoke as one by one the candles were extinguished. The cups were washed and left out.

'Should I dry these tonight and put them away?' Aelred said.

'I will put them away tomorrow,' Whim said. She had meant it sincerely, not unkindly, but the frustration in her heart came through.

'Mirth was right, little Whim. It's for the best.'

Whim blew out the last candle. She didn't say anything. She didn't look at her father. She went to bed. Moonlight filled her room and so did the sound of the breeze, the gentle blinking lights of fireflies outside the window. She regretted burning Elwyn's letter. Thinking of it now, it was just the brightness of his voice she heard. She could almost smell him, a smell like warm skin and acorn shells.

Whim sighed and turned over in bed, moonlight on her pillow. Lying there, Whim made a decision. Tomorrow, she would put the dishes away, like she had said. And then she would put on cloak and hood. She would follow the ralliers, stand with them. And if everything went the way she hoped, she would find her way to Elwyn. She would tell him face-to-face what was happening. She would bring him home.

# CHAPTER 11

# At the Station

IT WAS EARLY MORNING in late June when Whim saw the protesters off. The purple-pink haze was just inching into daylight as the Badfishians' singing voices faded to stillness. Those who stayed behind shook their heads from the windows and doorways, early-rising children's faces appearing smeared with honey. The protesters would march singing to Kegonsa and hop a train with the money they'd pooled to bribe a conductor to stow them in a freight car. They would don hoods and cloaks dyed red and walk in unison from the train station to the city hall in Liberty.

The hoods and cloaks were made from old sheets and tablecloths collected from houses around town and sewn by Aelred. Through the madder-dye, Whim could see specks of stains. She hastily folded her own protest garb into a cloth sack along with an envelope that had the Blackwells' address, then she slipped out into the woods. At first she went at her usual steady pace, but once she was out of sight of the town, she ran. She sped through the heavy underbrush of the woods she knew so well, that she could navigate as easily as any road. The course lay before her clearly: she would stay near enough to hear the sound of their singing, she would change her clothes, she would jump the train.

But as she neared the station, the wild raspberries – all well picked-over by children – grew thick and thorny. She stopped to wrap the cloak around herself in shadows and then fought her way through the thicket and into the open town. She pulled her red hood down over her face as she slipped into the crowd and watched her father, still hoodless, stand on a crate, his fiddle under his chin.

It was the final song. As the protesters sang it, clouds drew in from the west, the train came in. March Wilder walked up from Badfish Creek in his hand-pulled wagon to pick up the mail.

March went respectfully around the protesters, who were feeling energised and rowdy. He got the mail from the conductor and was pleasant and polite as usual. No one seemed to pay the postman any attention; their minds were too full of themselves. But just as March was leaving the station, some of the protesters at the back – Whim couldn't identify them with their hoods on – saw March and called out to him. They taunted, asked him why he wasn't coming along, knowing that he and his wife Janie were taking the money and leaving. Whim looked to her father, but Aelred was busy directing people into the freight car.

March acted like he didn't hear, just walked away at his usual steady pace. The men shouted after him, called him a traitor and a coward. And again, March ignored them.

So they went after him. The men began to push March a little. They snatched the sack of mail. Whim looked again to her father. He was talking to the conductor, making gestures to explain how everyone would fit into the freight car.

'Come on, now,' March said, a bit of worry in his usually even-toned voice.

'Stop it,' Whim said, approaching. 'Leave him alone.'

They barely glanced at her. One of the men dumped all the mail onto the road. March bent to pick it up and the man looked like he was going to push him to the ground.

'Stop!' Whim yelled again.

'You young gentlemen were about to pick up Mr Wilder's things before joining us on the train, isn't that right?' Aelred said, appearing beside her. After a moment's hesitation, the men did, stooping to the ground and collecting the scattered pieces. As March collected himself, Whim moved towards the crowd, hoping her father hadn't recognised her. But she felt a firm and gentle hand on her shoulder. She stopped. 'Little Whim.'

She turned to her father. She knew he was going to tell her to go home. Whim felt tears building in her eyes, tears of frustration.

'Don't think I am sending you back because I doubt your courage or your moral compass,' her father said. 'No one could doubt that. But you need to understand. History is full of the old generations sending the young to fight their battles. You don't need to carry this. It isn't your time.'

He looked at her, grieved. Defiance drained from her.

Aelred guided the rest of the protesters into the freight car, which was packed tightly with their red-clothed bodies, and Whim turned and walked back through the woods, grey and green below the heavy sky.

Not wanting to see anyone, Whim didn't follow the forest path. Instead she walked through the trees and the heavy brush, branches snagging on her red cloak. She was lost in thought when she heard a loud voice call her name.

'Whim.' Mirth walked toward her, heavy legs in heavy boots that crushed the spiny raspberries. 'Have you seen Dewey?' Her face was red with exertion or anger.

'Dewey?' Whim said.

'Stupid boy. He'll cause trouble, you know. If he's gone with those. . .' Her voice trailed off, as if taking in Whim's appearance for the first time; her cloak and hood. Mirth's face flashed for a moment with understanding, with pity. 'You wanted to join them?'

Whim didn't know how to answer. She would not lie. She stood still and waited.

'Whim, I have been meaning to speak to you.'

'What about?'

'I hope it's not too late. Seeing Dewey last night made it clear to me. I've raised foolhardy children. They need to be protected from themselves,' Mirth said. Whim looked at her cautiously. 'Whim, promise you won't tell Elwyn about the relocation. If he knows, if he catches a whiff of this, he won't stay there. He'll throw his whole life away.

He's smart but reckless, my boy. If he can just stick the course, he might actually make something of himself.' Her strong voice wavered as she spoke and the wrinkles between her eyebrows were deep. Worry made Mirth old.

Whim hardly remembered her own mother, but one image stayed with her through the years. Whim was five and had fallen from some high place, landing on her chin. There was a gash and a lot of blood. She ran to her mother. And her mother talked gently while she dressed the wound, using warm water and soft cloth. All the while, she had those same wrinkles between her eyes. The scar on Whim's chin remained.

Whim opened her mouth, then closed it again. She didn't know how to answer.

# CHAPTER 12

# Destiny

ELWYN AVOIDED further conversations with his aunt, and he avoided looking her in the eye for too long. He felt like her indifference to the world was a disease, one he was in danger of catching. There was no illness Elwyn would want less; for him, the chief virtues in life were enthusiasm, desire and action. Apathy was death.

A steely defiance grew day after day inside Elwyn's chest. Though his brain and schedule were full, as he sat through the long hours of study, he thought about ways to move forward in the life his aunt scorned. He wanted to do more, to throw himself at the things he wanted twice as hard. But he didn't know how.

Meanwhile, the longer Elwyn worked with his uncle, the more he began to doubt the plans laid out for him. Timothy's lessons were all about sitting, reading, following instructions, minding manners, memorising lines. How could such a closed, obedient training lead to the sort of life Elwyn wanted: one with not just riches, but also risk, adventure, good stories?

Wealth, Elwyn began to think, was not all created equal. Money was like good looks – what you did with it was the important thing. The Blackwells' money sat as unmoving as the well-preserved furniture that filled the unhappy house. Servants were paid, bread was bought, and nothing looked shabby or ill-kept, but modesty and conservation of resources ruled the day. Maybe this was virtuous, but Elwyn wasn't so sure. He wanted to go out and enjoy the life he had found himself in. He wanted to have a bit of money in his pocket, to buy an ice cream or a gaudy pocket handkerchief, or even just to wander by the shops and imagine that someday he could have everything inside.

'You're making excellent progress, Nephew,' Timothy said one afternoon, looking over the mathematics table Elwyn had completed.

'Yes, I know. And I hope you've noticed that I've been staying up to do the extra reading you recommended.'

'Indeed I have, and it is very well; diligence and obedience, Elwyn, are the most valuable traits a young man such as yourself can cultivate.'

But Elwyn brushed this compliment away. 'So I think you'll agree that I've done well enough to have some free time. Maybe an afternoon or two each week?'

'Free time?' Timothy said with distaste. 'What on earth for?'

'To enjoy.'

Timothy looked blankly at his nephew.

'You know – to explore, meet people, get some fresh air and exercise.'

'Nephew, I know that your upbringing was not one in which intellectual vigour was prized, but I cannot impress upon you enough the danger of idleness,' he said. 'Time, like all resources, must be submitted to structure, plans and procedure, or it will ruin you. Just think, for example, of the difference between your people and mine. I'm sure you must know *some* history? After the Second War, this country's resources were depleted, the population more than halved. In reaction, Foresters chose to live in idleness, without the structure of government or any other number of natural hierarchies. And what has come from the Foresters? What have their accomplishments been? Nothing. Some people think this has to do with breeding, but they are wrong. It's about structure. Unlike Foresters, people like you find here in Liberty took the chaos of the world and made order out of it. We erected towns. Built clocks. Split the land into parcels and elected leaders to govern with clarity and fairness. And that is why we have progressed.'

Elwyn was eager to object, but his uncle continued. 'And on the subject of governance, I've been meaning to speak with you, Nephew.' Timothy went on to explain that he had a role in country planning commission meetings at the city hall, signing papers, reviewing regulations, and other administrative tasks. He had taken the first few weeks of Elwyn's stay off to observe him and help him settle in, but he could no longer shirk his duties. Besides, his book proposal was already on its way to his old colleagues at the university press.

'But this time will not be wasted. I have your afternoon's studies well labelled and in the proper order. I am certain you will honour yourself and our work, and that you won't fall behind,' Timothy said. But Elwyn's mind was already far away. As he spoke with his uncle, new possibilities had crystallised in his mind, while other things had fallen away. He came to the realisation that no matter how long he worked according to his uncle's plans, he would never succeed in the way he wanted to. He would never succeed because he would be a part of someone else's vision, not his own.

Elwyn believed in enthusiasm, and enthusiasm dies if it's not cultivated. With his aunt's apathy in the back of his mind, Elwyn decided that he would honour that enthusiasm over the promise he made to his uncle. That afternoon, while his uncle was away, Elwyn would go back to that big white house on the hill. He would go there and convince Rhoad to give him a job.

After his uncle left, Elwyn sat for a few minutes at the desk to glance over the material left for him. And then, seeing no one outside but a robin, Elwyn opened the library's little round window. It was thick, built into the hill, and stiff with disuse. He crawled out into the grass and the sound of ticking clocks gave way to the sounds of the summer world: bluebirds, carts rolling on stone streets, women calling to one another, a man whistling as he brushed a horse tied to a post.

People muttered as Elwyn passed, but Elwyn hardly

noticed now. His mind was spinning with exhilaration and with all the words he might say to convince Rhoad to employ him or mentor him. And while he was at it, maybe he would catch a glimpse of that girl again, the girl with the goat.

Elwyn walked up to Rhoad's door and pressed the button that rang musical bells. He waited. Then he rang again. He heard shuffling footsteps inside and the same old woman answered the door.

'What are you doing here?' she said.

'I'm Elwyn. I don't know if you remember me. I brought back the goat a few weeks ago. I'd like a job,' Elwyn said.

She shut the door. Elwyn rang the bell again, and the door opened.

'Any job. If you'll just let me talk to Mr Rhoad about it. I'm a hard worker and can—'

'I have a house to keep and shopping to do. I don't have time to talk to charity cases that don't know their place.'

She shut the door again, but Elwyn was resolute. He rang the doorbell. When no one answered, he rang it again. And then again. That was when he heard dogs barking from the other side of the house. They materialised around the corner and ran towards him, teeth bared. Elwyn ran as fast as he could down the hill and over the river to the town centre, putting as many obstacles between himself and the animals as he could. But the dogs did not let up. Elwyn scrambled up a maple tree and sat for a good while until the dogs finally lost interest and began to trot back home.

It was only after they left that Elwyn's muscles relaxed. He looked out through the leaves, noticing for the first time where he was: in one of the few shade trees on the edge of the square, the train station on one side, the grassy city hall on the other, and shops and cobblers and dry-goods stores lining the way between. He could see the clock on the city hall nearing five-thirty, and his uncle stepping out for a break on the front steps with the other committee members, recognisable by their pale faces and over-buttoned clothing. Elwyn realised he wasn't sure when the meeting would end, and that he needed to get home before his uncle noticed that he was missing.

The men went back inside, but just as Elwyn was about to slip down the tree, he saw something else. The old woman from the Rhoad house *was* doing her shopping. A somewhat younger and bulkier woman led a horse with a small covered cart, and the old woman pointed and haggled while the younger woman loaded their things. Presently, the younger woman dropped a bunch of white turnips, and they rolled around the street like balls. The old woman, who Elwyn expected to yell and scold, instead bent down slowly, hand on her back, and helped the young woman pick up the vegetables. Elwyn looked at the clock on the city hall, then back to the women and the horse.

And then he jumped out of the tree and ran towards them, using the turnip distraction to climb into the cart undetected and hide himself below bolts of cloth. The basket of vegetables was placed on top of him and the cart began to move forward towards the house on the hill.

There, buried below cloth and turnips, Elwyn peeked through a crack in the side of the wagon. The sun reflecting off the river was blindingly beautiful, blindingly bright. When they reached the house, the cart was unhitched from the horse and unloaded in the servants' entrance. This was done slowly, as the groom was busy flirting with the young cook. Elwyn stole away into the house without any trouble. Inside he wandered without direction, trying to avoid being seen, lest the dogs be called again. It was foolhardy, and Elwyn knew it, but he also felt he had luck on his side. And perhaps he did, because not too far into his wanderings, he heard a sound coming from behind a closed door. It was a voice he recognised immediately for its assuredness, and Elwyn went closer, his heart jumping in his chest.

# CHAPTER 13

# *Riot*

'HESTIA, WHAT DON'T YOU UNDERSTAND?' Rhoad said. 'I am not running a campaign on merit. Nothing is about merit in this world. It's about stories. And what sort of story does it tell when the daughter of a candidate for the Chancellorship rolls her eyes behind him while he is giving a speech?'

'I wasn't rolling my eyes.'

'A photographer was there, Hestia. The one photograph of me addressing the people, on the front of newspapers across the Collective, and what is in the background? My loving family? No. My slightly intoxicated wife and my daughter rolling her eyes.'

'I think Mother looks nice. You can't tell she's intoxicated unless you know that she tilts a bit to the left after she's been drinking.'

'Hestia.'

'What do you want me to say? That I'll sit behind you with a prim smile and white gloves, gazing adoringly at you, every time there is a camera in the audience?'

'I don't think you understand what is on the line here. It isn't just my campaign. It's the future of the Collective.

You want to live in some backward country all your life? Or do you want to be part of moving the world forward?'

Elwyn thought this was as good a time as any to open the door. Cronus Rhoad looked slightly purple with exasperation, running a hand through neatly combed hair that was coming undone. Hestia stood in the centre of the room, feet planted, jaw set. She looked different than the first time Elwyn saw her. She had seemed sweet with her goat, but now defiance was her crowning trait; she inhabited every inch of herself the way small, strong creatures tend to do, the bees and the hummingbirds. The tips of her fingers, the ends of her hair were alive with an intensity that most people never reached, not even in their marrow.

'What are you doing here?' she said to Elwyn.

Rhoad now turned, looking calmer, but no more welcoming. 'Explain yourself,' he said. 'Who are you and what business do you have in my house?'

'I'm Elwyn, and—'

'It's the goat boy. The boy who brought back Willoughby,' Hestia said curtly. Her eyes, bright as a cat's and yellow-flecked, were scrutinising him.

'Well, what is he doing here?' Rhoad said, taking a bracing sip from his drink.

'I'm not a boy. I'm sixteen. And I'm here for a job.'

Rhoad put a manicured hand to his temple. 'You come into my private residence, unannounced, uninvited, and ask me to give you a job? Do you have any idea who I am?'

'You're Cronus Rhoad. I tried the front door, but your. . . that old woman wouldn't let me through.'

'Out,' was Rhoad's answer, turning his back to Elwyn.

'I can't—'

'Out.'

'I can't go until you give me a job,' Elwyn said.

'Out,' Rhoad said calmly, but his face was purpling again, and his lean height seeming to stretch taller. Then Hestia turned to the window.

'What is that sound?' she said. And despite the situation, they all quieted for a moment, because a noise could be heard beyond them, a sound outside the open windows, distant yelling. They went to look out and from their high, hilltop perch they could see the town square below filling with red-hooded figures.

'Hestia, stay here while I find out what's going on,' her father said. But Hestia was already out of the room and heading to the front door. Elwyn followed her, something in her drawing him. He felt a dangerous thrill, and instinctively reached into his pocket where he still kept his old sling. He had been taught since birth to always heed that instinct, to never be unprepared.

'Hestia!' Rhoad called out from the front door. 'Come back. Get inside.'

But she was running, and Elwyn started running, too, as they went over the river bridge. He didn't want to stop her, he just wanted to be there with her, to see what she saw. People from Liberty gathered in the park along the river – near enough to see the protest, far enough to feel safe. There was curiosity in their whispers, but more than that, there was fear, a fear Elwyn didn't understand.

It was nearing evening and the sun was getting lower, emblazoning the red of the protesters' cloaks and masks. There was something thrilling in the sound they made, in the red they wore. Elwyn and Hestia reached the group of protesters that was huddled around the town hall. They heard mutterings that someone inside had closed and bolted the doors. Elwyn caught a glimpse of his uncle behind the curtains in the hall window.

'This is the county seat, not just for the rich, but for all of us. We demand to talk to the people who signed these orders,' cried a man at the front of the mob. He stood on the steps and lifted his arms, igniting a roar through the crowd. The voice was familiar, but Elwyn didn't have time to place it. Hestia had disappeared, swallowed up as if by a great red shouting mouth.

Elwyn followed into a chaos of bumping and shouting that vibrated with life like a nest of field ants. The sound and the smell of the crowd – dew and campfire – filled Elwyn. His adrenalin was high as he pushed his way through, searching. He could hear Hestia's father's voice calling her name, just barely audible over the noise. But soon all other sounds were drowned out by the chanting of the crowd: 'Our lands, our plans! Our lands, our plans!'

People joined the man at the top of the city hall's steps. They pushed on the doors, and someone grabbed a large stick and began to bash the windows in. Elwyn couldn't hear the sound of them breaking, but he could feel it through the ground, like he felt the vibrations of the horses' hooves nearing in the stones below his feet. Between the jostle of people, Elwyn could see Cronus Rhoad climbing the steps of the city hall. Protesters were ramming the door. Rhoad seemed to be trying to say something, but like everything else, it couldn't be heard. The rattles and drums and horse sounds of the local militia joined the cacophony just as the doors to the city hall broke. The red people pushed in.

Elwyn stood on a bench, finally spotting Hestia's auburn hair in the sea of surging red. But from his perch, he saw something else, too. As the militia closed in, one of the people cloaked in red pulled out a revolver. He raised it above his head and shot it straight into the air, shouting something inaudible. Meanwhile the Hill people in the city hall were dragged out. Timothy was first, tears slicking his pink face as he was forced to stand. Elwyn's stomach churned.

The revolver was no longer aimed at the sky. It was aimed at Elwyn's uncle. And Elwyn, without stopping to think, grabbed a rock and put it into his sling. Within seconds, the stone was flying through the air towards the hand that held the gun, and hit it perfectly. The weapon fired as it dropped. Elwyn could hear a yell and saw Rhoad crumple as the misfired gun lodged a bullet in his foot.

Hestia ran to her father. Elwyn tried to follow, but between them the militia was beating the protesters. They fled, many with darker red stains on their red clothes. But as they ran, one of them stopped in front of Elwyn; the eyes, barely visible through the holes in the cloak, were wide.

'Elwyn. What are you doing here? Whose side are you on?'

But a militiaman came towards them, and the person who spoke to Elwyn vanished into the chaos of the crowd. Elwyn was kicked in the head – by who, he never saw – and collapsed on the ground. As he fell, it was the sound of the man's voice that echoed in his head, a voice as familiar as it was unplaceable in the mayhem that surrounded him.

# CHAPTER 14

# *Aelred Doesn't Come Home*

THE NIGHT WAS BALMY AND MOONLESS. A strong wind rocked the tops of the trees as the fireflies blinked and the crickets made their music. Whim was worried.

Sleep wasn't in Badfish Creek that night. When the wind paused, Whim could hear the stirring of people, quiet talk, rustling bedclothes. But it wasn't just the sounds. Sleeplessness could be felt in the quality of the air, thick as steam.

The wind picked up and it became harder to hear anything over the dark, waving branches. The fat-leaved oaks were the loudest of all, with their thickly knotted arms. A chill went up Whim's spine, and at first she didn't see the men and women that began to appear in the darkness, black figures in the black night. They were so quiet against the wind, she feared for a moment that they were ghosts.

'Allun!' she said, running to the first figure she recognised. He gave a half smile, but he didn't look happy. 'What happened? I thought you all would be home hours ago.'

'Ran into some trouble,' Allun said, uncharacteristically taciturn.

'Where's my father?' Whim said. As she got closer, she could see that half of Allun's face was puffy, a dirty cut from his cheekbone to his nose. Whim blanched at the sight. 'What happened? Where's my father?' she repeated.

'Allun!' Posy ran towards them, her hair tied up in curl-rags, trying to pull on boots as she ran. She cried when she reached him; tears rolled down Allun's face, too.

More protesters filtered in, filling the clearing where they usually gathered for fires. Their clothes were dirty, their legs dragging. Some were bloody, some had bruises darkening from yellow to purple on their exposed skin. Whim was frozen in place. It was as if she were a child, lost.

Dewey neared, clutching his hand and wincing with an urgency that woke Whim from her paralysis.

'Posy, I have a medical kit in the cupboard by the root barrel. Can you get it for me?' Whim asked, going to Dewey and examining his hand. Learning herbs and distilling from her father had also meant learning medicine – the two were woven together. Dewey's hand was swollen like a gourd and seemed to have bones shattered in several places.

Mirth came running from the Bramble house, holding a lamp. There was an alertness to her posture, like an eagle protecting its nest, and she quickly swooped towards her son.

**107**

'Somebody! Wake the doctor in Kegonsa!' she shouted, her face stony. 'Let me see that,' she said, reaching for her second son's hand.

'No.' Dewey pulled his hand away. Mirth grabbed it anyway, and Dewey, worn thin, acquiesced.

'You should never have been allowed to go,' Mirth said, anger boiling in her voice. 'Where's Aelred? He has to answer for this.'

'Aelred's in jail,' Allun said.

The words hit Whim with the force of a boulder. All the strength was knocked from her. *Aelred's in jail.* Her knees buckled. The dirt and leaves of the ground below her began to blur, and Whim nearly fell.

'Go get Neste and Enid,' she could hear Mirth saying. 'Whim is in shock.'

'No,' Whim said. 'I'm okay. I need to set Dewey's hand,' she said.

'We need a doctor,' Mirth said.

'I know what to do,' Whim said. And as the world around her regained its focus, she went through the contents of the medical basket – the herbs, house-made tinctures, splints, clean cloth – and pulled out what she would need. 'Why did they arrest him?' Whim said quietly to Dewey as she looked again at his hand.

'The militia came after us,' Dewey said, wincing in pain as Whim manipulated his muscles. 'I had brought my gun, which made them angry. They hate to see power in the hands of people like us. Don't look at me like that.

We had to defend ourselves, Whim. I thought they were going to kill us. But then Aelred stepped in. He took it all on himself. He said it was his gun. That he had shot it, but that he would say no more about who he was or where he came from until he got a fair trial.' Whim swallowed. 'Your father's an honourable man,' Dewey said, his voice becoming sharper. 'I wish I could say the same for my brother.'

'Dewey. . .' Allun warned, hovering nearby.

'Elwyn did this to me,' Dewey said. His face wasn't far from Whim's as she looked up from his hand.

'We don't know that, Dewey,' Allun said.

'I saw him. With his sling. I swear it, he did this to me, Allun. To his own brother,' Dewey retorted. 'You should have seen how he looked. Hill clothes. Short hair. Ridiculous.' Dewey sneered. 'What would Samuel Bramble say if he was looking down on us now? Samuel was born a slave and fought so we could live free on this land. Now one of his descendants is working on the side of people trying to exploit us.'

'Leave your brother out of this,' Mirth said, body tense. 'Are you sure he didn't recognise you?' There was something almost like desperation in her voice. But the sneer on Dewey's face grew, interrupted by violent flinches as Whim, who was listening gravely, put the splints in place.

'He's a traitor,' Dewey spat.

'Dewey, he couldn't have known—' Allun began.

'Couldn't he? What has Elwyn ever cared for but his own skin? His own grand life.'

'That's not fair,' Whim said.

'Answer my question. Did Elwyn recognise you?' Mirth said, voice low and growling.

'Elwyn again.' The pain and anger in Dewey's face had by this point blended into a perfect paleness as he looked up at his mother. 'You don't give a damn about this place. This place where our ancestors found safety after slavery, after the War. This place that fed us, that clothed us, that protected us. . .'

'I've given my sweat and blood to our life here. I have given up more than you could understand,' Mirth said.

'I understand that we are being stripped of the one thing that is ours. And all you care about is whether your favourite son will still get his little leg up in the world.'

Mirth slapped Dewey across the face. He didn't cower. He turned back to look at her. Mirth was tall: they met eye to eye. She spoke low.

'You're right. I do care about my children more than I care about this place. And I won't see them throwing their lives away for a hopeless cause or losing a chance to make something of themselves in this world. We are taking the relocation funds and going. And as for you, I won't have you going off and getting yourself killed by your own bullheaded recklessness. You won't be going off to any more of these rallies. We're going north to Hemlock

Draw to stay with your father's cousins. You'll come if I have to drag you.'

'I don't think there will be any more rallies, Mam,' Allun said gravely. The sun must have been about to rise – the sky was faintly light. But it was covered in clouds, and the birds hadn't begun to sing. Or maybe Whim just couldn't hear them. She still held Dewey's swollen, splinted hand. In her mind were images. Elwyn handing her his sling. Aelred being carried off to jail.

Whim went from person to person, cleaning cuts, applying poultices. When the doctor arrived from Kegonsa, there was nothing left to be done. It was mid-morning when Whim finished. The wind was still in her ears when she returned to her silent, empty house. She fell into a deep sleep, feeling, even as she slept, the absence that surrounded her.

When she woke, it was to the sound of screaming.

# CHAPTER 15

# Death

WHIM RAN OUTSIDE towards the wrenching sound. It came from the Wilder house behind the post office and little general store. Janie Wilder, the postman's wife, ran out the back door.

'He's dead,' Janie said, thick and pale.

She went back inside, and Whim followed. Janie's cries filled the small space. She was a reserved and tight-fisted woman, but her voice was like an animal. 'It was his heart,' Janie wailed. Whim couldn't look away from March, who lay ashen on the bed. Death wasn't foreign to Whim; it grew around them all, natural as the cattails in the marshes. But this scene felt all wrong – this man she had known so well unmoving in his bed. The sound of Janie's cries echoed in Whim like a drum.

'He was a sensitive man. It was too much for him, the stress of this relocation, these protesters mocking him, putting pressure on him at every turn,' Janie said, clutching at her own face. Whim felt dizzy. She had meant to come down to the post office that afternoon. She planned to talk to March about how to contact her father in jail. He was not only helpful, but also kind. And now, he was gone.

It was summer. Badfishians had the day to mourn, but only that. According to custom, the body was burned and the ashes made into a paste with water and smeared over the doors. People grieved for the quiet man, but also knew there was work to be done.

The town was sobered by Aelred's arrest and March's death – the two linked together in everyone's minds. When people talked about the protest, it wasn't in excitement. It had been dangerous. It had been a failure. It was what happened when you read too much, wrote to newspapers. It was what happened when you let yourself be foolhardy. Even the few people who still refused to leave town changed their attitude. Any grandness and idealism was gone. Everything was done quietly, almost in shame.

People wrote in to get their relocation funds. The literate helped the others and showed them where to put an X in place of a signature. Meanwhile, food stores were being cleared out and eaten, curtains taken down. No one sang while they worked, or whistled. No communal fire was lit. Nights were still and dry.

Whim wasn't leaving, but her days were equally full. With her father gone, she had to do his work at the distillery as well as her own. She had to lift heavy crates, roll barrels – work that kept her up late into the night and had her waking to an aching body at dawn each morning. But it didn't make her unhappy. If anything, it kept grief and worry at bay and helped her sleep at night.

What little spare time Whim had was spent at the post office, picking up her father's newspapers and waiting for a letter from him. She wanted desperately to write to him herself, but what Dewey said about Aelred keeping anonymous seemed to be right. Her father's face was sometimes in the newspapers, but his name and origin were never mentioned. Rewards were promised for anyone with information about his identity, and it seemed to be something of a fixation. The mystery gunman.

She didn't want to put anyone at risk by communicating with her father, but it had been two weeks since she had seen or heard from him. She had hoped he would find a way to let her know he was all right. The silence was beginning to weigh on her, and in those moments she wasn't working or sleeping, her chest felt tight, her breath restricted. She knew that the trouble might be as simple as unreliable post – she hadn't received any letters from Elwyn either – but she would feel much better if she could just get some assurance that her father was safe. Day by day, she doubted it more and more.

If March were still alive, these fraught moments getting mail might have been less traumatic. But as it was, Old Finchy, March's great aunt, now sat behind the postal counter while Janie took over deliveries and settled the accounts before moving. This surprised almost everyone, Finchy not being known for generosity. Janie forbade smoking in the store, but every time Whim went inside, Finchy had her long, thin pipe in her mouth, tobacco smoke pooling at the ceiling. Her black eyes watched Whim shrewdly. Day after day she looked on. When Whim asked if there were were any letters for her, Finchy shook her head with an air of futility and said, 'It won't do any good, you know.'

Though no letters arrived, Whim faithfully read the newspapers that came for her father. When Aelred was home, she had never bothered much with news from the outside world. Until recently, it all seemed unnecessary, a distraction from real things in life: flowers, roots, meals, seasons. But now those grey pages were the height of importance. They were a link between the woods and the world – the world was where her father was.

Whim searched for Aelred in the lines. Lists of what was known about this mystery gunman were prominent in every major paper from Hill Country. There were speculation pieces, plans for improved security measures in town centres. All of it Whim took in. She was hungry for anything that had to do with her father, anything that might help her understand what was happening.

Two weeks after the protest, Finchy handed Whim the newspapers with the same scepticism as always, but this time a weekly journal from Liberty was on top, one that Whim had never seen before. She felt a flicker of hope at the sight of it, and began to read right there in the post office. *Details Come to Light on Mystery Gunman's Past.* Whim perused the article for anything new, but it was the usual puffed-up speculation. Then halfway down the second page, her eyes lighted on words from a different article: *Timothy Blackwell and his Forester nephew.* Whim's breath caught in her chest. Timothy Blackwell was insisting that his Elwyn had not known the gunman and had not been involved in the protest.

> *'He is interested in the development of our society, not the destruction of it. That's why he came to Liberty. To seek an education. To distance himself from his unfortunate past. Now, my research indicates that if we just had a mandatory education programme for these underserved groups, we would no longer have a savage population at our doorstep, working in our fields. I will discuss this at length in my forthcoming book.'*
>
> *Critics of Blackwell's radical philosophy note that forcing Foresters into the education system would not only endanger students but would eventually take away from the available migrant workforce.*

Whim's eyes were glued to the paper even as she walked towards the door.

'One more thing,' Finchy said through lips still pinched around her pipe. Whim was so immersed in the pages, she had trouble understanding what Finchy was doing when she reached down and pulled a letter from below the counter. The address was written in a hand Whim didn't recognise, but when she opened it and saw the familiar writing inside, tears began to fall even before she read the words. Finchy didn't comfort her, but sat looking on, smoking. There in the store, Old Finchy staring unpleasantly, Whim read the letter over and over.

*Little Whim,*

*You must be worried, but there is no need for that. I have been given a cell, food and water, and should receive a trial date any day now. I cannot lie to you and say my days are pleasant or altogether free of violence. But any pain inflicted on me is nothing compared to pain I would feel looking in the mirror each day after doing nothing to defend my home or protect my people.*

*The only regret I have is leaving you, dear little Whim. I hope beyond all reason that my trial will be soon and will be quick and will return me to you. The truth, I still believe, will prevail. But until we are reunited, I have consolation in your deep kindness and your capacity for mercy. There is more in those two qualities than any militia, any foolhardy boy with a gun. Who could feel hopeless while there is a girl like you in the world?*

*I've enclosed the address of a friend I have made here. He will see your letters get to me and mine to you. Meanwhile, be assured that I am caring for myself as best I can. I am thinking of you often, loving you constantly, and am always,*

*Your father*

As she read on and on, again and again, her tears grew heavier, louder, harder to wipe away. Dappled sun streamed into the room that smelt like tobacco smoke, wax and glue and sugar bins. And Whim felt life in her body, as if she had been holding her breath underwater and had just come up for air.

'Thank you, Finchy,' she said.

And Finchy said, 'You're welcome.'


When Whim finished crying and stepped outside, everything had gained a sharpness: the untended gardens, untrained pumpkin vine, the smell of dry dirt on the wind. It was a quiet time of day; mothers napped after a long morning packing and young people cooled themselves in the creek. Whim returned to the stills, bottling, testing, barrelling through the heat of the day. But the work didn't feel as heavy as it had before. Her hands had become more capable as the days went on, her arms stronger. Whim's mind, for the first time in so long, felt free. And it was in that freedom that an idea grew.

When the supper hour neared, Whim went to the creek to wash the sweat from her body. Rising from the water and dressing, she saw a curl of smoke and heard humming ahead. Finchy lived down by the creek and was home tending her bees. Whim hadn't forgotten what the old woman had once said about her father, nor had Whim forgiven it. But she also remembered a small tenderness in Finchy's voice that afternoon, and the way the letter had been set aside. Whim went towards the sound of humming, hair dripping down her back and soaking her clothes.

'I hear you, girl,' Finchy remarked as Whim approached, not turning from her bees. 'Well? What do you have to say? Just standing around doesn't suit you.'

Whim wasn't bothered by what Finchy said. She doubted anything could bother her just then. What made Whim pause was the sight through Finchy's open window. The lace curtains were still hanging. The lace cloth over the table. Everything was in its place.

'I thought you were leaving with Janie Wilder next week. You haven't packed your things,' Whim said.

'Of course not,' Finchy said. 'And I expect you haven't either unless you've lost your nerve.' Finchy turned away from the bees and removed her gloves. 'I'm about to pour a cup of mead for myself. I suppose I can pour two.'

'Are you sure you want to share your table with the daughter of a troublemaker?'

Old Finchy raised her eyebrows. 'He made a mess, you know, of his great "resistance".'

'Nothing good ever comes neatly.'

'You still stand by your foolish father, then?'

'I always stand by what's right.'

Finchy looked at Whim appraisingly. Then a flicker of cold humour flashed in the old woman's eyes.

'Come in for that cup of mead.'

Whim followed and sat on one side of the lace-covered table while Finchy sat at the other. The old woman took out two ancient crystal glasses and poured a stingy glass of mead for herself and then a stingy glass for Whim. They raised their glasses and drank. In all these years, Whim had never tried mead. Aelred had always described the local home-brewed liquors as 'coarse', but this was delicate and dark. It warmed Whim's insides like they had been cold. Finchy stared at her. It seemed to Whim that everything was being inspected by those small eyes.

'I'm planning another protest. Continuing the resist-ance. . .' Whim said.

'You're a foolish girl. Like your father.'

'I want you to help me.'

# CHAPTER 16

# Isolation Is a Fortress

THE AWFULNESS OF THE DEMONSTRATION had faded like the pain where Elwyn had been hit on the head. The bullet aimed at Timothy had hit Rhoad's foot, but the wound wasn't deep. One life, at least, had been saved. When Timothy heard what had happened, he looked at his nephew with what seemed to be real tenderness, maybe even respect. Elwyn thought this might be a turning point for him in Liberty. He imagined stepping out on the streets and hearing people whisper in tones other than the suspicion that he had almost grown accustomed to. Maybe people in town would even admire him.

Above all, Elwyn hoped that a turn in public opinion might mean Rhoad would change his mind and give him a job. Elwyn understood that his actions had not only saved lives, but may even have saved Rhoad's campaign. Rhoad was running on progress, and fear makes people want to buckle down, close their doors, not open them. Maybe he would get a letter from Rhoad, apologising for the lack of welcome, asking Elwyn to help him with his work. The whole thing seemed like it could be a bizarre stroke of luck.

But the morning after the protest, the headline of the newspaper wasn't *Ambitious Young Man Saves Uncle*. On the front page, right below *Mysterious Gunman Fires During Protest*, was a story with the headline *Forester Wields Weapon*. '*He carried it in his pocket*,' the paper quoted a townsperson as saying. '*A sling. All this time he's been carrying it around with him. It makes me afraid to walk in my own town. Who knows what might set these people off.*' Elwyn thought it must have been a mistake, but the next day the paper said much the same, and again the next day, until Elwyn had no interest in the news. He took care to avoid the papers and all talk about the protest. But still he heard things. People talked about it incessantly, the 'June 28th Protest'. It was in the air like the cottonwood fluff. Foresters marching through town, masked, cloaked in red. As word spread, the supposed numbers of Foresters grew from a couple dozen men and women to hundreds. Politicians began to talk about it. Tomison Garreth, Chancellor of the Central Territories and Rhoad's political opponent, spoke about it regularly.

'*This is why the isolation we have cultivated is so essential to our way of life*,' a newspaper quoted Garreth as saying. '*Isolation is a fortress against anarchy. The anarchy that threw our people into chaos, violence and destruction eight-score years ago. The anarchy that rears its head now and, for the survival of our Collective, must be kept back.*'

Timothy tried to continue with Elwyn's lessons as before, but hate-filled letters started pouring in, and diligent Timothy wanted to answer them all, defending his position with academic terms and references to the studies and bodies of work he admired. Elwyn wasn't sure this was the way to respond – the letters were full of emotion, not reason, and in Elwyn's experience, people didn't listen unless they were spoken to on their own terms. Elwyn tried telling that to Timothy, but he was always hushed.

It was twelve days after the protest that an X was burned with strong-smelling vinegar into the grass that covered the Blackwell house. 'Burn the Trash' was painted on the door in red. Timothy turned pale when he read it, but Boaz smiled. Timothy had been jittery since the protest, startled easily by loud noises.

'Boys, go to your rooms while I call the police,' Timothy said.

'I give it a week before my father realises how much trouble you are and sends you back where you came from,' Boaz whispered to his cousin as they walked down the hall.

'What have I ever done to you?' Elwyn said. But Boaz ignored him, going into his room without giving his cousin so much as a glance. Elwyn stood in the doorway of the room, where things were organised in neat rows by size. The week had taken a toll on him, and he didn't want to be unheard. 'I asked you a question,' he said. Boaz turned to face his cousin, his face going a little pink like his father's. *This is it,* Elwyn thought. *We will finally have it out, he and I.*

'Are you really that stupid? You *being* here is the problem, tree trash. Do you know what people are saying about my family? Now that they know we are related to people like you?' The sneer was gone from Boaz's face. It looked serious and almost scared. 'I told my parents things like this would happen if they took you in, but they didn't listen. My father only cares about his work, and my mother doesn't care about anything. It's up to me to look out for the reputation of this family. I can't count on anyone but myself.'

Elwyn, who had prepared to channel his disappointment and confusion into an argument, found the anger drained from him. It wasn't lost on him that Boaz, though hateful, hadn't sent him out of his room, hadn't shut the door in his face.

'I knew this man, Otis, who lived up in Kegonsa,' Elwyn said. 'He was the skinniest, smallest man around, and he was afraid of everything. He didn't go on hunts because he was afraid of getting caught in a trap, he didn't go fishing because he was afraid of falling into the water, and he never said a word to the woman he liked because he was afraid she wouldn't like him back. And when people asked him if he ever planned on getting married, he said what you just said. "I can't count on anyone but myself."'

'What are you talking about?' Boaz said, looking even more irritated at his cousin.

'See, one day Otis's brother teased him so much that he finally agreed to go fishing. And would you believe it, he was so lightweight that when a large fish pulled on his line, Otis was pulled right into the water. The fish dragged him around the lake half the day, and he didn't dare let go because he couldn't swim. Of course, people gathered around watching. They thought about helping, but Otis wasn't in real danger, and there's not much entertainment in the woods.'

'Shocking,' Boaz said spitefully.

'It was after lunch when the line broke and Otis struggled his way to the shore. And you know what he did then? He went straight up to that girl he had his eye on and proposed right then and there, his clothes still sopping wet. And she said yes. Not only that, but she was so happy, and he was always so eager to treat her with this or that good thing to eat, that she got fatter and fatter and became one of the largest women you've ever seen. And because Otis had his wife's weight by his side, the man wasn't afraid of fishing any more, or of anything else.'

'Are you telling me this to try to *help* me?' Boaz said.

'We all need help,' Elwyn said.

But Boaz was angry now. He moved to the door. And before he shut it, he spat on his cousin's face. Elwyn wiped his cheek, disgust rising in him. He banged on the closed door with his fist.

'What is wrong with you?' he yelled. Boaz was leaning against the door to try to prevent Elwyn from entering, but

Elwyn threw his weight and shoved it open. Boaz stood, looking well pleased with himself, and Elwyn, for the first time, really did want to hit his cousin. But Foresters never fought people weaker than them. Years ago in Badfish Creek, it came out that Victor Page was hitting his wife, Laura. And all the Forester men in town – and any women who were stronger than Victor, too – lined up at his door and one after the other gave him a punch to the jaw.

'You know, I used to want to meet you,' Elwyn said. 'When I heard I had a cousin out in Hill Country, the same age as me. I used to imagine we'd meet someday. Become friends.'

'I never wanted to meet you.'

'You've made that clear enough. So maybe you don't like me. Some people don't. I don't care. But you have six other cousins in Badfish Creek you haven't met. And an aunt. Each of them is worth ten of you, and you don't even care if you ever meet them.'

'Oh no, you're wrong. I do care. I would rather cut off my own right hand than have any more tree trash showing up on our doorstep for the whole world to see. Asking for favours.'

Their voices had grown louder and louder as they talked. When Elwyn heard Timothy rushing down the hall towards them, he thought their fight was the reason. He looked at his cousin's defiant face before turning to his uncle. He thought maybe Boaz was right, and his fate with the Blackwells was being decided right there. But when Timothy appeared around the corner, his face was shining with perspiration and happiness.

'Elwyn,' he said, breathless. 'I've just received a telegram. My publisher will be here tomorrow to discuss something with us.'

'Is that good?' Elwyn said.

'"Is that good?" This protest, this opposition, may be the best thing that could have happened. I'll admit I was getting worried. But, you see, all this attention you've drawn to us and our project. . . my publisher must think it will drive up interest in my book. I think he's going to ask if we can release the book sooner than planned.' Timothy glanced at his son. 'Don't slouch, Boaz. It reflects poorly.'

Timothy ate three helpings of dinner that night and half of the massive strawberry cake he asked the cook to bring out in celebration. The joy was infectious. Elwyn found himself caught up in it; even Piety gave what seemed like a heartfelt congratulations to him and his uncle, wishing them both luck. It was the first time Elwyn had seen his aunt and uncle looking happy together. They seemed elevated by the possibility of good news: hope has a way of transforming all people. Only Boaz was untouched by the lightened mood. His sulking had an air of the sinister.

The next day, Timothy had Elwyn bathe in water and buttermilk, dress his best, comb his hair. But when the publisher arrived, he hardly glanced at Elwyn. He was a grey, discerning man.

'Timothy,' he said gravely. 'May I speak to you in private?'

# CHAPTER 17

# Tree Trash

WITH THOSE WORDS, all the happiness was let out of the room. The clocks were the only sound. Timothy's face went dull. He led his publisher to his office and closed the door. Elwyn followed and pressed his ear to it.

'I'm sorry, Timothy. It's been decided,' the man said.' Due to recent events, we've decided times are too contentious for this sort of work. If our university wants donor support—'

'But surely you saw the efficacy of my methods.'

'Efficacy has nothing to do with it. People are afraid, Timothy. They're hearing stories about a mob dressed in red invading their square. A Forester with a sling, a wild man with a gun. No one wants to financially support a university that puts out a book detailing how to bring these people into society.'

'It's just a flash in the pan. It will all pass by the time we get this book polished and ready for distribution,' Timothy said.

'There is no "we". There is no collaboration here. No partnership.'

'But after all we've been through, Jared.'

'That was a long time ago, Timothy. A long time ago. I came only as a friend. Only to let you know before you waste too much of your time on this little project.'

Elwyn winced at the word 'little'. He waited for his uncle to defend himself and his work, but Timothy was silent. The silence tugged at Elwyn. He hated hearing his uncle so helpless. So weak. He couldn't leave him like that. Elwyn opened the door.

'Hello.' He extended his hand to the publisher. 'I'm Elwyn Bramble. We met a few minutes ago at the door.' The man looked confused and hesitated a moment before shaking Elwyn's hand. 'And I want you to know that this isn't just a little project. It's groundbreaking, and really important at a time like this. Isn't that right, Uncle Blackwell?'

Timothy stood silent, red.

'I can recite the first few lines of Virgil's *Georgics* for you. In Latin. I don't really understand it yet, but I'm getting better—' Elwyn continued.

'That's enough, Elwyn,' Timothy interjected.

'Or Seneca, maybe. My uncle just had me start memorising *De Constantia Sapientis*.'

'I'm going to go now, Timothy,' the man said, returning his hat to his head and moving towards the door.

'Wait!' Elwyn stepped between the man and the door. 'You're missing a great opportunity. An opportunity to be on the right side of history,' he said, parroting his uncle.

'Elwyn, I said that's enough!' Timothy shouted, spit flying from his pink face. Elwyn was surprised into silence.

The publisher stepped gingerly around him, keeping plenty of space between their two bodies.

'I'll let myself out, Timothy. Send the boy back to the fields. Let him be with his own people. Where he belongs.'

The door shut, and Timothy grabbed Elwyn by the scruff of his shirt. Timothy wasn't strong, but anger filled him, his eyes wild with rage. At first Elwyn was sure his uncle was going to hurt him, pull something off the wall and send it crashing over his head. But instead, Timothy dragged Elwyn to his room, pushed him in, and locked it from the outside. Elwyn was too shocked to resist.

'You will learn not to open doors you have not been invited to open.' There was a lack of restraint in Timothy's voice, and, for the first time, a raw, untethered emotion. His vanishing footsteps were as rapid and heavy as Elwyn's heartbeat.

Elwyn could hardly believe what had happened. He kept waiting for his uncle to come back and unlock the door. The light outside Elwyn's window lost its harshness. Time ticked on. It was nearly sunset when Timothy returned. He spoke through the locked door.

'I don't see any reason for us to carry on with the project. Your time here has come to an end,' Timothy said, the heavy wood muffling his voice, but not enough that Elwyn couldn't hear the current of anger still running through it.

Elwyn had been sitting on his bed, channelling his frustration into a piece of string and a series of complicated knots Allun had once tried to teach him. He had been handling the injustice of the last couple weeks with what he thought was patience, even grace. But this was too much. He walked to the door to be sure he was heard.

'You don't see any reason to go on?' Elwyn challenged.

'I will make arrangements for you to return on tomorrow's train.'

'I've done everything right. Everything you've said, I've done. I followed all your rules. I read all the books you told me to. Did the exercises. And do you think I wanted to? No. But I did it anyway. I did it because you're my uncle, and you helped me when I asked for help.'

'You disobeyed me. You should have been at home working, not at the protest,' Timothy said, getting pinker.

'That gun was aimed at you. I saved you.'

'You opened us up to scrutiny!' Timothy's voice boomed with a strength Elwyn didn't know his uncle was capable of. He could feel the wood vibrate. Then hush came over the room, punctuated only by the ticking clocks. Elwyn thought for a moment that his uncle had gone. 'You'll leave tomorrow. That is final,' Timothy said quietly, before his footsteps once again echoed down the hall.

Elwyn was alone in the quiet. The room wasn't as big as it had seemed when he first arrived. The stacks of books on his desk, the papers and pencils that had seemed to keep him captive now looked innocent, such a small price to pay for the life he wanted. Why hadn't he kept his head down, done the work he was asked to do? Why did he compulsively stick his neck out and try for something more? Why couldn't he just be content with what he was given, like everybody else?

Elwyn lay on his bed and looked at the ceiling as the sun grew dim and twilight neared. He felt drained of energy, drained of himself. But then just a spark of that old fire flashed in his chest. He rose to his feet, moved a chair to stand on, and began to work at the skylight frame with the letter opener from his desk. He prised at the glass and wood until it finally loosened, and Elwyn lifted the window and pushed it aside, then crawled onto the grass.

The evening was starless and heavy with clouds and heat. Fireflies still flourished in the fields. Gas lamps in the town were being lit, twinkling in their glass cages, and at the front doors of inns and houses. Elwyn turned away from the centre of town, towards the river and the hill to the north, where the Rhoad house perched like a giant lantern, its many windows alight against the blue-purple sky.

He knocked on the door, but no one answered. When he knocked again, the door opened, but this time it wasn't the old woman. It was Rhoad himself, weight on his left foot, a crutch under his arm.

'Oh. It's you,' he said, looking past Elwyn for a moment, as though he was expecting someone else, someone who might appear through the half-light behind him.

Elwyn was surprised to see Rhoad. He had thought the maid would come, would make fun of him and let the dogs out. This stroke of luck bolstered his confidence. 'I need to talk to you.'

'Here to ask for another job?' Rhoad's clear, authoritative voice sounded harsh in the stillness of the night.

'I have a proposition for you.'

'Is this going to end in my foot getting shot again?' Rhoad said, the soft light casting deep shadows on his handsome face.

'It's about your campaign. I've heard it's in trouble.'

'You acted courageously. I see that. If it weren't for your actions, a man may be dead, and the situation I find my campaign in could be even worse. Thank you. Now, go home.'

'I think you should hear what I have to say.'

'I understand things aren't pleasant for you. You acted boldly and instead of being rewarded, all people see is a Forester with a sling in his pocket. That is just the way these thing go sometimes. It is not fair, but it is human nature. I have myself and my own affairs to think of. This protest has voters terrified. They're flocking to Garreth. I don't have time for your problems, I'm busy enough with mine.'

'That's why I'm here. I have an idea for how I can help.'

'And I'm sure this is purely for my benefit. No self-serving motives.' Rhoad's sarcasm was as dry and hard as the stone steps where Elwyn stood.

'Of course I have self-serving motives. That's what business is about anyway, isn't it? It's an exchange that works out for both people. Otherwise it's not business, it's swindling.' Rhoad didn't invite Elwyn inside. He studied him, and Elwyn looked directly back. 'I understand your situation,' Elwyn began. 'I read about you in books, how you got to where you are. You took risks. You never balked. You and I have that in common. I also believe in being bold when things get hard,' Elwyn said. 'Doubling down. Not sitting around complaining about a bad foot, hoping things get better.'

That was when it began to rain, a fast, heavy rain that poured out of the sky all at once and turned into warm gold where it was touched by the gaslight. The water drenched him, but Elwyn didn't move, and Rhoad still didn't invite him in. The two of them stared at each other.

'I want to be your campaign assistant,' Elwyn said, raising his voice to be heard over the downpour. 'Everyone will expect you to put as much distance as possible between yourself and folks like me, but you'll never be able to play into people's fear the way Garreth does. You aren't about self-protection. I've read your speeches. You said we have to "let go of old baggage to free our hands for the building a new future". So why are you running a campaign the same way everyone does?' Rhoad's face did not change as he listened to Elwyn.

'Taking me on as an assistant, taking me on publicly, would surprise everyone. It would get people talking.

Maybe they wouldn't all be saying great things, but at least you would be directing the conversation, not the other way round. It would be the turning point in your campaign. The moment you stopped talking about a new Collective and started living it.'

Rhoad studied Elwyn a bit longer. 'Well. Come inside,' he said.

Elwyn stepped out of the rain and into the brilliance of the Rhoad house. He wasn't wrapped in a blanket or even given a towel to dry off with, but that didn't matter. Elwyn was bathed in the light of hundreds of flames reflecting off hundreds of glass crystals and mirrors. And he knew instinctively that he had punched through the ceiling. That he was on his way up.

# CHAPTER 18

# A Familiar Face

IT WAS MORNING before Elwyn returned to the Blackwell house. Rhoad wanted to hear the specifics of Elwyn's campaign ideas. He was a man dissatisfied with generalities; ideas should be clear, strong and stand on their own feet. After that, tireless Rhoad wanted to negotiate the terms of Elwyn's employment – his title, hours and wages. By the time they finished, it was nearly two in the morning, and a place was made for Elwyn in a guest suite.

Though it was late, Elwyn was not tired. He wasn't hungry either. He lay in bed and felt the oxygen moving through his veins. He felt the sparks of connections in his mind; he felt pride. Elwyn felt fully alive in a way he hadn't for a very long time.

The guest room was unlike any Elwyn had ever entered, but it felt familiar to him. It was a place that had lived in his imagination for years: the sprung mattress, deep silk sheets, crystal lamps, gilded wallpaper. Somehow it was all even brighter than the picture he had held in his mind, and he was comfortable there. Happy.

When Elwyn finally fell asleep, it was in a state so exhilarated that when he woke a few hours later, he was completely refreshed. Rhoad was working, but coffee and buttered white-flour rolls had been ordered for him and set on a tray beside his door. The taste was still in Elwyn's mouth as he walked down the hostile streets. But none of the looks or words shot at him touched Elwyn at all. They rolled off his back like rain off a goose.

'Uncle Timothy?' Elwyn shouted when he entered the Blackwells' house, not minding the rule against shouting. It was breakfast hour. Elwyn burst into the room, bright and breathless.

'You're late,' Timothy said, not looking up.

'I spent the night at the Rhoads',' Elwyn said, his pleasure doubling at the looks his aunt, uncle and cousin wore when they looked up at him. 'I'll be working there now. Earning money. I'll be able to stay somewhere I won't – what is it you said? – open you up to scrutiny.'

'Elwyn, last night I may have been too hasty. There are perhaps other publishers to whom I can present my project. To align yourself with someone like Rhoad. . .' For the first time, Timothy did not speak easily and abundantly. There were no little lessons tagged onto his words.

'I'm going to some boarding houses this morning. Some won't want to admit a Forester, but Rhoad has given me a note promising that I'm good for the money. I only stopped in to let you know.' Elwyn felt radiant as he spoke. He had possibilities open to him that no one else could have planned for him, no one else would have thought possible.

'So that's it? You will so easily abandon your lessons? Abandon the future you vowed your devotion to?' Timothy said, flaring with the same anger Elwyn had seen the day before.

Boaz seemed to be in a mixed state of delight and displeasure – delight over his cousin leaving, displeasure over the terms. But Piety's face, for the first time, showed a glimmer of something beyond its usual composure. What she was feeling, Elwyn didn't know, but it wasn't happiness.

'Timothy,' she said gently. Timothy tried to compose himself by staring at the table, then shovelling a spoon of sugared porridge into his mouth, his hand shaking with suppressed anger. 'I would like Elwyn to continue to stay with us,' she said keeping her eyes on her nephew. Unlike her voice, her eyes were not gentle. There was something persistent, almost pleading in them.

Timothy threw down his spoon. 'We had an agreement! If he stays, he must live in accordance with it!'

'I know how important rules are to you,' she said 'But I can give you all kinds of reasons this new arrangement may benefit you. Letitia Rhoad's family ownership of several presses out in St Louis. A greater audience for the book. Less fear from people uncertain about endorsing your work. But I'm sure that you will think of all these things in time yourself, and they don't matter to me. What matters is that this is my nephew. I have promised to keep him here. And I *like* having him here.'

These words didn't exactly make Elwyn happy. In fact, some of the buoyant pleasure drained from him. He had liked the idea of leaving the house victorious, and he knew he wouldn't leave if his aunt wanted him to stay. As fraught as his feelings towards her were, he still felt bound to her in some way. He still loved her.

'If you stay, and if you take this position' Timothy said, 'we will have to create some conditions.' But there was a change in Timothy's face. Elwyn could see that he was beginning to think about his book again, about his work.

'That's right,' Elwyn said, turning back to his uncle. 'We will. But I'm not helpless, you know. I'm willing to stay and assist you with your book, but things need to be different. I've agreed to work with Rhoad from early morning to noon five days a week. I can work two hours with you in the afternoon – and I'll work hard – but I need to have some leisure time every day to enjoy myself.'

'Elwyn, idleness. . .' Timothy began, but then stopped himself. 'Three hours.'

'Two and a half.'

Timothy sat silently for a moment. The clocks ticked. Then he nodded, almost imperceptibly.

'Well, Elwyn. I will have some notes and the book proposal prepared for you to pass on to Letitia,' he said more serenely as he scooped another spoon of porridge. Piety gave Elwyn what was almost a smile while Boaz stormed out of the room.

*

If Elwyn expected a change in his aunt's manner, he was wrong. In the days that followed, Piety practised her usual sceptical reticence, moving in her own set of unseen friends and engagements, sitting in her private parlour. This disinterest confused Elwyn. At the dinner table, Elwyn often found his eyes going to his aunt, hoping for a sign of approval, a sign of *something*.

'Well, and how was your first day assisting Cronus Rhoad? Please, share the details with us,' Timothy asked over a lunch of salads and cold tongue. Elwyn had only just returned to the Blackwells' and had a quick wash; the dazed satisfaction of the day still filled his mind.

'It was note-taking mostly. Mr Rhoad likes to have someone there to jot down ideas while he's busy with other things – eating breakfast, organising papers, that sort of thing. He says the morning hours are the most productive, and most people don't use them well.' Elwyn ate heartily, but between bites he glanced at his aunt to see if her face betrayed any thoughts. She cut at her food with no more interest in the conversation than Boaz had.

'There is sense in that, no denying it,' Timothy said, with his usual happy effort to find Rhoad agreeable, to find the whole new arrangement to his liking.

'Then we went through town on an errand to get people accustomed to seeing us together. It was drizzling and I held Rhoad's umbrella for him – that was my idea. I figure if people are afraid of Foresters because they think they're dangerous, I should show myself being the opposite. Being kind. We're doing the same sort of thing in the campaign – making sure I'm shown being helpful so people are less scared.'

'Sensible, sensible.'

'Rhoad thinks that Foresters have an important role in the Collective, and once people see that, we'll all be better off. After the walk, some men from the campaign press arrived from St Louis, and I brought out the tea and some sweets for everyone. It was a huge tray. There were at least twelve types of chocolate.'

'Extravagant, I'm sure. . . but I suppose allowances should be made for guests.'

'They invited me to sit with them and we had a nice time. I even told some stories about Badfish Creek, one about when Dewey and I were little and tied our sled to the big buck that wandered around – we called him Old Smokey because he was so sagging and grey. They all laughed. They said they thought I'd be a great asset to the campaign.' Elwyn felt excitement welling up in him as he said these words, and again he looked at his aunt and again he was disappointed.

'And did you deliver my proposal? And my note to Rhoad concerning your continued schooling? Does he have any suggestions for a track we should take that might be of more interest to his wife's publishers? I'd be happy to incorporate his ideas into our project, especially if he would like to assist in its promotion—'

'He read the message. He said he's sure that whatever you are doing is fine.' Elwyn spoke absently. He wasn't certain why his aunt's disinterest bothered him so much. He wasn't used to being troubled by the opinion of others. But Piety seeing the merit in Elwyn's work felt essential to him. It felt like a matter of good versus evil, truth versus falsehood, light and dark.

That night, he got out of bed. He took the jam Piety recommended from the pantry, and the cheese and slices of bread to go with it. He knocked on his aunt's parlour door and when she answered, he held out a sandwich.

'I heard you like a midnight snack,' he said. She raised an eyebrow, but invited Elwyn in. She had been sitting in the glow of lamplight, with her newspaper and book beside her along with a pot of tea, her carefully selected paintings and portraits looking on. 'I want to talk to you about something,' Elwyn said after he sat down.

'Really?' Piety said in mock surprise, taking a bite of her sandwich. 'Well, then. Go ahead.'

But Elwyn's words failed him. He stumbled trying to explain. 'I want you to know what it was like to work at Rhoad's today. There were times it was a little uncomfortable, you know, the way new things always are uncomfortable. But even then, it was just right. It was like that feeling when you are running really fast, and it takes no effort at all – you could just keep going and going.'

'I'm pleased to hear it,' she said drily.

'No. I want you to really understand. The first day I

stepped into that house, I knew I wanted to be a part of that world, no matter how hard I had to work for it. But after talking to you, a part of me, a small part, was afraid I would be disappointed if I got what I wanted. But I'm not disappointed. It's the opposite. It's like, not only does everything there shine, but under every shiny layer is something bright and interesting. They have these candies and they're wrapped in foil – all different colours of foil. And inside is hard candy and in the middle of the hard candy is something like rose sugar that melts in your mouth, liquid peppermint, or a cherry soaked in brandy. It's like that. And Rhoad. He looks rich and has nice clothes and good manners, but below that, he's also so smart. He's thought everything in his life through, from the tiniest little bits of his day to the big ideas about history and the world.'

'So this is what you want to talk about, Elwyn? Your infatuation with the life of that family?'

'You said I'd find out that the things I'm aiming for in my life are empty,' Elwyn said. His face was flushed; he could feel his pulse in his arms. 'You were wrong. One scratch below the surface and you can see that there's depth to everything. You must have felt that sometime. About something.'

Elwyn was ardent and sincere in this and thought his plea would have to touch his aunt's heart. But she only set down the sandwich and picked up her newspaper.

'Just when I was very young,' she said. She held the paper high, and Elwyn could no longer see her frown. But he saw something else. There on the front page of the paper was a sketch of a familiar face. Elwyn rose, drawn to the image of Aelred Moone.

TRIAL DATE SET FOR MYSTERY GUNMAN

# CHAPTER 19

# Gumption

THE FIRST STEP to people treating each other well is really seeing each other. Whim believed that. That was why the protest she planned was such a strange one.

One goal was to free her father, to storm the jail, break down cell walls. That part was straight forward enough. But Whim had a mind that understood the importance of subtleties; she went on resisting the village relocation with an understanding that what you do isn't quite as important as how you do it. The last protest had failed, and Whim believed this was partly because of the way they had been dressed. Red masks and anonymity were intended to make an impression, and they did. But they also stirred up fear, and fear distanced people from one another.

The next demonstration was scheduled for the 30th of July. That was three days before Aelred's trial, and three was a holy number, a number that meant wholeness. There would be no cloaks, concealments or costumes. Protesters would come as they were. And Whim didn't want just the usual people to come, the bold and fire-bellied. She wanted everyone: young and old, dark and light, able and ill, tired and cheerful. She wanted the sort of people who rarely left their homes, people who were afraid, people who were cynical. She wanted the whole spectrum of Foresters to march through Liberty because she wanted every person looking out their windows to see someone like them in the marching crowd.

There needed to be a lot of people to achieve the effect Whim wanted – many more than the last time. That was where Old Finchy came in. Whim could recruit certain folks well enough on her own, but Finchy's circles were wide and deep-rooted. By virtue of her years, Finchy knew many families in the woods, and her age, history and relative wealth made her someone people revered, especially those less impressed by manners.

Whim should have been surprised that Finchy agreed to help her, but she wasn't. Ever since she got that first letter from her father, it was like there was a wind at her back. She sailed through the long days of keeping up with the distillery and organised the protest, making pamphlets, sending messages, talking to everyone she could.

Aelred's trial was scheduled for the 2nd of August, the same date the final relocation was scheduled. Men would come and forcibly remove the remaining people from Badfish Creek, forfeiting all compensation. Whim had discussed this with her father in their letters. She felt sure that it was illegal to seize lands this way, but her father had lived longer and was more cynical about the shape of the world. He said that there was a private backer for the project who claimed presence in Badfish Creek was dangerous to the future of the Collective Homesteads.

'*Is it possible, then, that by disproving this claim in court, we could regain the rights to our land?*' Whim wrote to her father.

'*Reading your believing words does me good, little Whim. But show me a time that courts have sided with a handful of Foresters over wealth interests. I'm afraid we have to find a different way.*'

She did not write to her father about the protest she was planning – she couldn't risk the letters being intercepted. Anyway, Aelred seemed to take some comfort in his daughter's safety. He instructed her, when the time came, to go with the Brambles. He would find her afterwards, and they would work to regain control of what they'd lost. Whim refused to lose anything. She wanted it all.

Late every night that hot summer, Whim had to wade into the creek to rinse off the sweat and dirt that coated her body. By the time she got home to her bed, she would fall immediately asleep, and when she woke, her brain was full of the day ahead. Those moments in the creek were the only time her mind had a chance to wander its old familiar paths. As well as wondering if her father was being treated well, if he would be proud of her, she also found herself wondering about her old friend Elwyn. When his name came up during the day, Whim felt anger rising inside her. It wasn't an anger she thought was just – he had done nothing wrong that she could think of – but emotion doesn't bow to reason. At night things were different. At night and in the water.

Elwyn didn't write any more, nor did Whim write to him. She had no news from him to think about. Her thoughts just went to old memories, treasured and dear: when Elwyn fell out of a tree trying to chase a squirrel and she helped him limp home, when they tried to teach each other to waltz but neither knew how to lead, when they sat on summer nights eating walnuts by the creek.

Memories like these stood in Whim's mind as she dipped her head down under the moonlit water. The movement calmed her aching muscles, and though she was tired, she didn't want to leave. She made her way towards the bank anyway, knowing that morning always came quickly. On her way she heard laughter and running. Enid and Neste splashed into the water, Neste with her easy grace, Enid like a happy dog. When she saw Caradoc leap after them, Whim sank lower in the water. They were fully clothed, unlike Whim who was in her underthings. The stream tugged and moved the fabric as the three romped loudly, splashing each other and laughing until they tired themselves.

'I can't believe this is our last week here,' Enid said, dropping down in a shallow place and letting the current go around her. 'You're so lucky you don't have a mother like ours, Caradoc. I'd give my right leg to go with everyone else to march into Liberty and get Aelred out of jail. I don't know how Whim did it. Everyone was so set on just leaving with their money. Now there's only a handful of people who aren't going to stay and rally together.'

Caradoc was cupping handfuls of water and bringing them to his face to wash it. 'Everything she said was true,' he said, between cupfuls. 'It's worth sticking your neck out for what's important. And besides, between Finchy and Whim Moone, they've got the trust of pretty much all the woods. Whim might not have sway the same way Finchy does, but I've heard plenty of people say she's the real reason they are joining up. An honest girl won't lead you wrong.'

'Yes, yes, I know. I hear it all the time. Whim gets to be brave and inspiring, while here I am just cleaning and packing, cleaning and packing,' Enid said.

'You're strong, you have a head on your shoulders. Why don't you just tell your mother you'll be staying behind to march with us?'

'She likes to talk about it, but doesn't have the gumption,' Neste piped in, wringing out her hair. 'Oh, don't be offended, Enid. I like you with gumption or without.'

'It's not that. Gumption I've got. I'm spitting mad at Mam, but Allun's leaving with Posy's family and now Dewey's going with him. If I leave, there'll hardly be anyone left with her.'

'Do you believe what Mam says?' Neste asked, dropping her voice a bit lower.

'What? That trying to get Aelred out of jail will just stir Hill people up against us and hurt the cause? Who cares? We'll do what's right or die trying!' Enid sighed a disgruntled sigh. 'Or I *would*, anyway.'

'I saw a letter Mam got from Aelred the other day,' Neste said, dropping her voice even lower.

'Aelred? She shouldn't be writing to Aelred,' Caradoc said easily. 'We're supposed to keep things quiet.'

'What did it say? Don't tell me you didn't read it,' Enid said.

'Shh. Of course I read it. I'm sure Mam wasn't too explicit in her letter – she's smart enough. But from what I read, it sounded like Aelred knew that something was in the works, something being led by Whim.'

'What did he say?'

'He told Mirth to keep Whim with her, to keep her safe. To not, under any condition, let her risk her safety.'

Whim was still for a while, quietly letting the words soak in. She hated the idea of other people conspiring to keep her safe when she didn't want safety, not for herself.

'Whim Moone will find a way,' Caradoc said.

Enid sighed heavily. 'Maybe I don't have gumption.'

'At least you're here,' Neste said. 'Not off with Elwyn, living with the people who fought Allun and put Aelred in jail.'

'I'd give my right leg to see Elwyn's face when he sees everyone marching through Liberty,' Enid said, this time with a bit of a laugh in her voice. 'Do you think he'll join in?'

Whim didn't hear what they said. She quietly made her way over to the shore and climbed out of the water.

# CHAPTER 20

# *Trust*

THAT WEEK BEFORE THE MARCH, Badfish Creek was in a state of anticipation. The first families were leaving and being given their farewells. Some farewells were warm, others were accusatory. Having lost her husband so recently, everyone understood when Janie Wilder shut down the post office and sold off the goods in the store; Mirth, meanwhile, was considered nearly a traitor. People stopped by to tell her so as she worked, and she brushed them off like a large animal brushes off a fly with the flick of their muscles.

For those who stayed, excitement bubbled as the day of the protest drew near. People packed sacks for the two-day walk to Liberty – they would start in the morning, make camp, and arrive midday of the 30th. The fires lit were bigger than Whim had ever seen before. There was a lot of singing, too. Finchy said her bees wouldn't do well without her, so she would stay behind and keep things in order. In the meantime, everyone was well supplied with her mead.

And maybe it was the mead or maybe it was the common goal they all shared, but aside from the usual skirmishes there was no real discord. Old disputes faded, quarrelsome siblings quarrelled less. There was an odd peace and a sense of purpose that prevailed in the woods.

But though everyone was happy, Whim was more eager than ever for the preparations to be over and the march to begin. She was afraid that something might keep it all from happening. She walked down stony paths carefully to avoid twisted ankles, and she took elderberry tinctures to avoid illness. She kept away from the Brambles, and whenever she saw Mirth, Whim felt as alert as a young rabbit. And like a rabbit, her fear only made her quicker. Her work was done with more speed and agility than ever.

Every few days, on top of her preparations and tasks at the distillery, Whim walked to Kegonsa, where she now had to go if she wanted to pick up her newspapers and send word to her father. As usual, no letters arrived from Elwyn. She thought perhaps he had become too wrapped up in money and new clothes and had forgotten about her, but she decided long ago not to dwell on it. The bitterness was acute, and she had no time for bitterness.

Whim had no time for anything, really, not even newspapers. She carried them home in a pack over her shoulder and read as she walked, having few opportunities to just sit down. She walked and read, sun slanting through the shivering cottonwoods.

One day, turning the page, she was surprised by an image. She dropped the newspaper, and it landed face up to show Elwyn's eyes looking at her, smiling. Wind in the high branches of the trees didn't reach the ground;

the newspaper was still as if it had been carved in stone. Kneeling down over the paper, Whim was almost afraid to touch it. She thought that her imagination, her repressed anger and anxieties, were playing games with her. But no. There he was. Elwyn.

She picked up the paper and quickly flipped through it. She saw another image, then another. They were advertisements, at least one of them in every paper. There were many editorial cartoons mocking it, too. One had a group of Foresters with various skin tones and invariably gaudy clothing – large hats, massive bows – shaking hands with Rhoad, their high-buttoned shoes crushing miniature Hill farms beneath them. *The Rhoad to Disaster.*

It took some time before she got to the headline buried in the *St Louis Times*: *Injured Rhoad Takes Forester as Campaign Assistant.*

Fire flashed from her feet to her chest. She dropped down where she was and read through the stack of newspapers until the words began to blur, and then she read some more. It was then that she reached the odd sections, ones she normally didn't pay attention to. Business. Finance.

TEN YEARS AFTER INTRODUCING BONDS,
COLLECTIVE RESOURCES COMPANY ON THE RISE

*'We are opening several new sand mines this year,' says owner and aspiring Central Territories Chancellor*

*Cronus Rhoad. 'Not only will this utilise under-utilised land and labour force, but it will set the Collective on a path towards modernisation.'*

Whim sat up taller. She read the article three times, read it furiously. She knew that business interests were behind the seizure of land, but business interests had seemed like a faceless force in the world. She had never put a name to them. And here was a name. Rhoad. The man Elwyn had admired all this time, and now, apparently, was working for.

Whim hurried back to town, for what purpose, she didn't know. She just felt an urgency in her, urgency with no outlet.

'Teilo! We are not bringing a skunk with us to your uncle's,' Whim heard Mirth say as she passed the Bramble house. Mirth had leant her weight over the side of their wagon and was lifting a stack of blankets to reveal another hand-made cage, this one holding a comfortable look-ing skunk. 'It's a long enough journey without getting skunk-sprayed.'

'Mike won't spray us. Skunks only spray when they're scared, and he knows we won't hurt him. Mike's a really trusting skunk.'

'No more animals. How many times do I have to say it? This cart will be heavy to drag across the forest without stowing away an entire menagerie. You're lucky we're let-ting you bring that filthy bird of yours.'

'You didn't say no animals. You said no rodents when you found Roger under the pans.'

'Roger?'

'My groundhog. Skunks aren't rodents. And neither are opossums.'

'Teilo,' Mirth warned, before diving back into the wagon, her large bottom in the air, eventually finding the caged opossum below the store of dry breads. 'If I find one more animal. . .'

As she went by, Whim kept one eye on Mirth. She kept waiting for her to act, to speak, but so far, Mirth hadn't. Instead Mirth, like Whim, was constantly looking out of the corner of her eye. They seemed to orbit each other, bound by mutual love and distrust.

'Hello, Whim. Back from picking up your papers, I see,' Mirth said as Whim went by. She tightened the wagon ties roughly. 'Have you heard from Elwyn?'

Whim stopped. 'No,' she said. She tried to keep her voice even.

'He must be very busy. If anybody can make the most of an opportunity, it's Elwyn.'

'That's right.' Whim swallowed, turning to walk away.

'Wait,' Mirth said. There was a change in her tone. 'Whim, I need to talk to you. Privately.'

Whim turned, afraid and relieved that the confrontation she had prepared herself for was finally coming. They went to Whim's house. Whim poured lukewarm sun-tea and brought out chips of ice while Mirth sat, looking uncomfortable, like she always did when she wasn't working.

'Whim, I wanted you to know that I've been in correspondence with your father,' Mirth finally said. 'I was a farm girl when I lived in Hill Country. I don't know much about the legal system. But I wanted to offer him whatever advice I could.'

'And that's all?' Whim found herself saying. There was a harshness she didn't intend in her voice, but Mirth didn't seem to notice.

'I also wanted to give him some idea of what you have been up to. A parent can't watch a child deceive another parent. It's not right.' Whim waited, knowing Mirth was about to say more, wondering what she would try to do or say to make her go with them. For a moment, the two of them were quiet. Then Mirth continued hesitatingly. 'As you know, Neste, Enid, Teilo, Loew and I will be leaving tomorrow,' Mirth said. 'Your father asked me to promise that you would come with us. But I could not do that.' Whim could feel her own heart beating in her chest. 'You are like a daughter to me, and as with my own children, I have a bias towards your safety. But if it were my own father facing a trial that could cost him his life, well, I could only hope I'd do just the same as you are doing.'

At first Whim didn't understand what Mirth was saying. She had been too braced for the opposite. Then Mirth smiled with a rare gentleness.

'What I'm trying to say is, I'm proud of you.'

# CHAPTER 21

## *Legacies*

ELWYN BEGAN HIS JOB as Cronus Rhoad's assistant in mid-July, and ever since, his life should have been saturated with colour, like old cloth dropped in a vat of dye. Elwyn was given a new wardrobe of good linen expertly cut in colours that looked good on his brown skin. And he got to stand with Rhoad for portraits, photographs and interviews. The coffee they drank wasn't dandelion coffee like they drank back home, but real coffee from Mexico, and the cakes were flavoured with things Elwyn had never tasted: nutmeg, saffron, vanilla. Everything smelt good and was served on gold-rimmed plates in the glittering parlour. The air itself seemed brighter there, full of life and interest.

But Elwyn had seen Aelred's face in the newspaper, and he could not unsee it. The image stayed with him, all morning every morning as he worked. He tried asking Rhoad questions about it, but Rhoad said that all he knew was that this gunman, identity unknown to all, claimed to have led the violent demonstration at the city hall and to have fired the gun that hit his foot.

'And that's the man's picture?' Elwyn asked more than once that first week.

'The trial is on the second. You can go and see for yourself then, if you are interested in that sort of thing. They aren't letting anyone into the jail to look at him – they claim that's for public safety. But if I know Garreth's campaign, he's pulled some strings to arrange it that way. Nothing keeps a story in the papers like a mystery, and every reminder of the protest is a free advertisement for his backward ideas.'

'So how do we know that's him?'

'Thinking too much about this mystery gunman is only playing into their hands, and is pointless. The courts will do their work. I don't waste my time with things that don't serve me, and I suggest you do the same.'

But every day after work, Elwyn haunted the jail behind the courthouse. He wasn't alone; there was always a crowd of a dozen or so people trying to catch a glimpse of the man through the slats in the window. Petty thefts and incurable drunks usually filled the jail, but now there was an assassin from the woods, one that some folks said wanted a revolution. People stood out in the heat of the day, swapping gossip and buzzing with excitement over the ever-nearing trial. Elwyn tried getting close to the slats in the wall and calling out, hoping Aelred would recognise his voice. A moment from the protest replayed itself over and over again in Elwyn's head: a cloaked man had asked Elwyn whose side he was on. A familiar voice. Aelred's.

If Aelred heard Elwyn through the slats in the jail wall, he never answered.

Elwyn didn't notice how people in the crowd looked at him any more. The question didn't interest him – he had a million others always bubbling in his mind. Why was Aelred keeping his identity secret? Could Elwyn tell anyone that he knew him? What would Aelred have been doing at the protest? Why would Aelred, who hated guns, have fired one?

It all seemed wrong to Elwyn. He wrote again and again to Whim and to his family for answers, putting his sealed and stamped letters, as usual, in the brass mailbox at the front of the Blackwell house. But Elwyn never got any reply. He began to doubt what the newspapers said. If Aelred was in jail, someone surely would have told him. What if the courts didn't have *anyone* to blame for that gun at the demonstration? What if the rioters all got away, and they needed to pretend they had someone to hold account-able. They could just circulate a picture, say he's too dangerous to be in contact with the public. At the last minute, they could make the trial private, say it's for public safety.

Elwyn had been spending his mornings around politicians and newspaper men. He understood that this was often how things worked for people like that. Rhoad's words about Garreth influencing the courts for his own politics echoed in Elwyn's mind. Every day, he doubted Aelred's presence in the Liberty jail more and more. But he felt he had to know for sure. He had to find a way.

Elwyn spent hours walking around the jail, inspecting it from all directions. He missed lunch with the Blackwells more days than not, but he hardly thought about that. He had a bit of money in his pocket from his work with Rhoad and any time his hunger became a bother he bought a roll filled with sausage or sorrel from a vender. He ate absently as he thought, walking around the jail again and again.

He was buying one of these rolls when he felt a tap on his shoulder.

'Hello there, goat boy,' Hestia said coolly, but in good humour. Elwyn saw Hestia almost every day now – the family was always sitting around the breakfast table when Elwyn arrived – but he and Hestia hadn't ever really spoken. She was groggy-eyed and irritable in the morning, and after breakfast she disappeared to work with her tutor. It was different seeing her out in the world. She stood with the ease and energy of a small flame.

'Hi,' Elwyn said.

Hestia looked at the roll Elwyn had chosen and wrinkled her nose. 'The beef is much better, you know,' she said, thanking the vendor and paying him for her roll.

'I can't eat beef,' Elwyn said. If this encounter with Hestia had happened a couple weeks earlier, he would have been transfigured with joy, but now Elwyn was more eager to get back to the courthouse and find a way inside.

'Can't?' Hestia said. 'I'm suspicious of people who don't eat delicious things.'

'I promised my brother I wouldn't eat any cows while I'm here. I used to walk him down to the train tracks to watch the cattle cars pass through – you could hear the moos and see a few noses and shadows through the slats, but not much. He was really happy I was going to a place where cows lived until he heard that people kill and eat them. And he's just six, you know, the youngest of our family. It's always hard to say no to the youngest.'

Hestia looked at him as if what he said was completely foreign. Elwyn felt that she was appraising him, her eyes narrowing as they looked him over. It was the first time since he arrived in Liberty that he felt he was being judged as a person rather than a Forester.

There was a noise back by the jail; people cheered, then groaned collectively. Elwyn whipped around in that direction, but there was nothing to see.

'Don't tell me you're wasting your time on this ridiculous trial. *The Mystery Gunman*,' she said in a mocking tone.

'What do you mean?'

'It's always the same. People do everything they can to keep danger out of their lives, then when something terrible actually happens, they tear into it like starving dogs.'

'That's not how it is for me.'

'Oh, of course not,' she said.

'You're just like your dad. "Don't put time into what doesn't serve you."'

'I'm nothing like my dad.'

'No? Well, anyway, this *does* serve me. For me this is personal. It isn't about thrill-seeking. It's about family.'

Hestia took a bite of her bun and assessed Elwyn more closely. They were walking around the square aimlessly, or so it seemed to Elwyn. The sun was bright, but the day was fresh with clouds the colour of moth's wings. He looked back at the jail again, which was now blocked from view. He was tired of carrying all the questions in his head alone. He wanted to talk. He wanted to be understood.

'The man whose picture they have in the paper, the man they say is going to be tried as an assassin – it's my best friend's father. Whim. She's like a sister to me, and I've known her dad all my life. I haven't told anyone—' Elwyn began.

'Nor should you.'

'But it can't be right. He'd never do something like that.'

'You can't know that. People are usually capable of more than you think, for better or worse.'

'None of it makes sense. Aelred never liked guns. He always complained they were loud and ugly. And then also, no one has really seen who they have in jail. And I haven't heard anything from anyone back home. . .' Elwyn's voice trailed off as he looked back at the courthouse again. 'I just need to know if it's him. If he's really there.'

Hestia looked at him thoughtfully for a moment. 'What difference does it make to you?'

'"What difference does it make"? It makes all the difference. I mean, if he's in jail, then I have to do something.

I've got to find a lawyer or find a way to prove he's innocent or. . . I don't know. Something. And if it isn't Aelred, then everything's all right. I'm hoping they don't have anyone at all, but just picked a random name and picture.'

'That's all right to you?'

'Sure.'

'You'd be fine with the leaders of this country, the courts, the law-enforcers, lying? You don't mind them manipulating citizens to believe what they want them to believe as long as the people you know are okay?'

'Well, I don't know. That's just politics, isn't it? They might have good intentions, at least some of them.'

'Oh, might they?'

'Yes. I mean, I'm sure there are bad examples here and there, but there are plenty of people like your dad, too.'

'Well, that I can't disagree with,' Hestia said with a cynical laugh. 'There are certainly plenty of people out there willing to sacrifice honesty for their own personal ambition. Most of them just aren't as good at it as my father is.'

'That's not what I meant.'

'Yes, well, you're a very good assistant to him, aren't you?' she said, clearly displeased, though Elwyn wasn't sure why or where the conversation went wrong. He just knew he didn't want to be arguing.

'Listen,' he said, trying to start over, 'have you ever had ice cream?'

'Of course.'

'I haven't. I got close once. When I was twelve, this woman in my hometown had a big party for her ninetieth birthday. Old Finchy, we call her. People came in from all over the woods and she bought whisky, sheep for roasting, and a bunch of milk, cream and ice. She mixed the milk and cream with big chunks of honeycomb from her hives and had us all take turns churning it in buckets to make ice cream. But she said it was a celebration of age, not youth, so people would be served oldest to youngest, and the old folks had appetites, let me tell you. By the time we kids got to it, all that was left was the melted bits of cream and honey in the bottom of the bucket, and we passed it around and licked it clean. Anyway, I've wanted to try ice cream ever since I got here, but no occasion seemed right. Until today.'

The cynicism had softened a bit on Hestia's face. 'What's today?'

'The day we became friends. Unless you think I'm too good of an assistant.'

If there was a hint of a smile around the corners of Hestia's mouth, she tried not to show it. 'You're buying?' she said.

'Of course.'

The two of them got ice creams in paper dishes and walked for a while, Elwyn talking about about Aelred and Badfish Creek, Hestia talking about the girls' boarding school where she had spent most of her young life.

'I miss it. I'd be there another year still, before going to university, but they pulled me out so I wouldn't miss campaign events. Boarding schools and distant daughters aren't popular with the working people,' Hestia said. Her father had told Elwyn the same thing, but when Rhoad said it, the idea seemed practical. Now it seemed cruel, using logic like that on another person's life.

'Why did you tell me about your friend's father?' Hestia asked. 'I could tell everyone. I could make things worse. Why do you trust me?'

'I don't know. But I do. Am I wrong?'

The heat rose from the stone below them, melting the ice creams. Hestia's was charlie-mint, Elwyn's black raspberry.

'Think about what I said. About what it means for the powerful to deceive the people they serve,' Hestia said, taking her last, melted bite. 'And I'll be thinking about the situation with your friend's father.' Once again, she looked at Elwyn, assessing him carefully.

'Goodbye, Elwyn Bramble,' she said and walked away.

# CHAPTER 22

# The Man in the Cell

THE NEXT MORNING, life went its usual way. Elwyn woke early, bathed and set out through the sleeping streets to Rhoad's house on the hill. The weather was humid, as it usually was, and in Rhoad's office, the wet air was filled with the same smell of Mexican coffee. Elwyn wrote while his boss dictated, he filed papers and then, once finished, he joined the family at the breakfast table. When Elwyn had first started, a place had been made for him in the kitchen with the servants, but Rhoad put an end to that.

'Don't be silly,' he'd said. 'He is an assistant, not a servant. He will sit at the far end of the breakfast table. Besides, what if something needs attention? I hate to lose time in the morning.'

The change had pleased Elwyn. At the Rhoad table, Elwyn felt he was where he belonged – a part of this beautiful family, in a room with glass and mirrors, light coming in from all directions. The room was quiet, but not a quiet like at the Blackwells', full of clocks, history and dust. The quiet at Rhoad's house held a sense of anticipation. The large windows of every room looked out at the world. Elwyn always felt possibility there.

But though it was ordinary in every way, that morning felt different to Elwyn. Not only was he anxious about Aelred's presence or non-presence in the nearby jail, he was also preoccupied by the things Hestia had said the day before. He had been kept awake by her words most of the night, and in the morning they still set a dull cast over everything. Elwyn kept looking over at Rhoad, thinking about the way Hestia had spoken about her father, wondering if she saw something he didn't. But Rhoad, uninterested in subtleties of mood, sat at the table as usual, devouring three newspapers, a soft-boiled egg and grapefruit. Now and again, he would run across a sentence that he wanted to remember, and he'd say it out loud for Elwyn to write in a notebook he kept beside his plate. Hestia, too, seemed her usual self. She did not make an effort to communicate anything to Elwyn nor reassure him.

But when breakfast was over, she slipped a note into Elwyn's pocket.

*By the jail. Two o'clock.*

\*

Elwyn arrived first. He ate a quick lunch, answering as succinctly as possible his uncle's usual questions about the work Elwyn had done that day and giving self-assessments of his progress in several areas. Timothy also asked again about the prospect of Rhoad endorsing the book once it was published – something Elwyn thought was unlikely. Piety asked a few questions about the work, too, ones that Timothy didn't realise were tongue-in-cheek. Elwyn was too preoccupied to be troubled. He didn't even notice his cousin wasn't at the table until he got up to go.

'Where's Boaz?' Elwyn asked.

'He signed up for some sort of class, didn't he, Piety?'

'Chess, I think,' she said. 'He'll be away for lunch a couple of days a week.'

'Chess, excellent choice,' Timothy said. 'Where are you going?' he asked, seeing Elwyn rise. 'I was hoping I could give you a test in penmanship. We have so often missed your formal exercises, but I'd love to see if simple note-taking has a similar effect on improving your hand.'

'Sorry. I have something I need to do for Miss Rhoad. Hestia,' Elwyn said, walking out before the meal had finished.

'Of course, duty calls,' Timothy said, a little despondent.

Elwyn's pulse rose as he turned to the door, went out into the bright midday sun and towards the jail. As he neared, he went faster and faster until he was almost running.

'Have you done like I said?' was the first thing Hestia asked when she arrived some minutes later, skipping any greetings. 'Have you thought about what it means for leaders to manipulate the people they serve?'

'I have. But I don't know what I think.'

'Good. Thinking is what matters. The problem isn't that most people are bad or stupid, the problem is that they don't think things through. Anyway, I'm sure if you keep mulling things over, you'll see that I'm right.' Hestia didn't seem to be assessing Elwyn any more. Whatever her thoughts were about him, they seemed to be quite settled, for better or for worse. 'Here,' Hestia said, handing Elwyn a bag with boxy things inside. 'It's two cameras, with the flash and film – everything's ready. If we get in, we'll need to take pictures of what we find there, of the empty cells, if that's the case. Of course, the courts will just say they temporarily moved him, but it'll get people questioning, and that's the biggest step.'

Hestia hopped up the stairs two at a time with the athletic grace that characterised her movements. Elwyn followed behind. She handed the guard a letter from her father and talked to him with a confidence that amazed Elwyn, even as his stomach began to tighten and tighten. He wasn't accustomed to fear, but he feared this. He feared finding out that Aelred was in jail for something he did, and he feared finding out Aelred was in jail for something he didn't do. Now he also wouldn't be satisfied if the cell was empty. But of all these, the thing he feared most was not finding out the truth. The guard re-read the paper once more before letting them in.

'Why didn't your father come himself?' the man asked, unlocking the gate.

'Oh, I love helping with my father's work. I just hope I can be a little bit like him someday. I'm sure you understand – you have daughters, don't you, Mr Timidy?'

When they got inside, the guard told them to wait there while he talked to his supervisor.

'I thought you didn't believe in lying?' Elwyn said.

'*Leaders* lying. To the people,' she said. 'Come on. The high-security area is just down these steps. It's only padlocked.' The deftness of her mind and movements was impressive as from her bag she took out a metal block and with one swift, silent swing, broke the lock. 'Come on. We need pictures of every cell and the empty room as a whole before anyone notices we're here.'

But of course, the secured room was not empty. In it was a cell, and in that was a man. The man was someone Elwyn didn't recognise in the dim light. He was hunched, lean and swollen.

Then Aelred looked up through his tangled hair.

'Well. The Brambles' golden boy has finally come to visit.'

# CHAPTER 23

# *Choices*

MEMORIES FLOODED ELWYN at the sound of that voice.
Over the years, he had heard Aelred singing around the
fires at night, talking to Whim about distillery expenses,
whispering to his young daughter as he carried her home.
But there hadn't been bitterness in his voice then, not like
there was now. The bitter tone, the dirt in his hair, the
patches of yellow and purple on his face that Elwyn was
beginning to see – it all was deeply disturbing. The room
seemed to be getting smaller around Elwyn, and his chest,
too, felt cramped.

'Aelred. What happened to you?'

'I should be asking you that same question,' Aelred
replied, looking disdainfully at the clothes Elwyn wore,
his newly trimmed hair and clean, well-fed face.

'Are you okay? We have to get you out of here,' Elwyn
said, trying to pull at the bars as if they might come loose.

'I've accepted my fate. I will speak the truth, stand for
my people and accept the consequences.'

'Stand up for what? Consequences? I don't understand.'

'Of course you don't understand,' Aelred said. 'All
your life, it's been the same. You walk through your days

not seeing anything beyond yourself. Well, look around, Elwyn. This is as real as the fine clothes on your back.'

'I'm not the enemy here. I want to help you. I want to fix this,' Elwyn said.

'Of course you want to fix this. If I'm here, beaten and bloody in a jail cell, you can't think your new, shiny world is as lovely as you want to think it is. You need to get me well and back home so you can feel good again.'

'That's not why I'm here. I don't think it is. And. . . what does it even matter?' Elwyn said, his chest becoming even tighter. 'What can I do to get you out? To help?' Elwyn turned to Hestia. 'Hestia. You've got to talk to that guard again. Maybe—'

'Elwyn, this man is on trial for an assassination attempt. I can't just talk them into letting him free.'

'Hey!' the guard yelled. 'How did you kids get in there?'

'Elwyn, come on.' Hestia tugged at him.

'You get out of there,' he yelled.

'I'm not leaving,' Elwyn said. 'I know him. Aelred, tell him I know you. This is a mistake.'

'No one comes in here but this man's lawyer,' the guard said.

'I suppose his lawyer was the one who left that bruise on his face?' Hestia said.

'Out.'

'I'll let Whim know where you are. I'll let her know you are safe,' Elwyn said to Aelred as the guard pulled him by the arm.

'Leave my daughter alone. She doesn't need your help. She knows where I am. Everyone knows where I am. You haven't bothered writing to her in a long time, and I'm glad of it. Don't let this change anything.'

'Aelred. Tell him you know me,' Elwyn said. He could feel the blood pulsing through the veins in his fingers, hear it in his ears. He yelled to the guard. 'That man doesn't belong here. He's not—'

'No,' Aelred said, composed but without gratitude or familiarity. 'You are the one who isn't where you belong.'

After they left, Hestia smoothed things over, somehow, with the guard, but Elwyn didn't know how. All he could hear was his own pulse in his ears and the thoughts speeding through his mind. He hadn't gotten word from anyone back home for almost a month, and from what Aelred said, they hadn't heard from him either. The afternoon air was hot and bright outside the city hall. Everything seemed wrong, but there was one thing Elwyn latched onto: someone had been tampering with his mail. That person, Elwyn felt, was to blame for Elwyn's ignorance, and for Aelred's disdain.

At that moment, Boaz appeared in the square. He was clearly not at a chess class. He was with some friends, laughing, and when he saw Elwyn he walked over to him, bold and sneering. 'How sweet. Hestia Rhoad's taking her pet for a walk again. The goat was better looking.' Boaz's friends chuckled behind him.

'How dare you—' Hestia began, but Elwyn had already lunged at his cousin, taking them both to the ground. Elwyn put his arm across his cousin's chest, forcefully pinning him. 'Where are my letters? What did you do with them?'

'Your letters?'

'The ones I sent home. The ones that came for me.'

'I don't care about some tree-trash letters.'

Elwyn pushed down harder, and Boaz groaned. His friends weren't helping him; they and others had gathered round in a circle, watching. 'I don't have your letters.' Boaz choked as he talked.

'They were full of important things. If I had known, I could have done something. I could have helped.'

'I didn't touch your stupid mail.' Boaz choked again. This time, Hestia pulled Elwyn off.

'I think that's enough,' she said.

Reluctantly, he let his cousin up.

'You'll get in trouble for this,' Boaz said, rubbing his chest as he walked away, the little crowd that had formed dispersing.

'Hestia. I am going to be gone for a day,' Elwyn said. 'Two at most.' He turned and started for the train station. His hands were empty, he had no bag, but that didn't matter. All that mattered was getting home.

'Elwyn!' Hestia called after him. Her voice saying his name sent a ripple through his body, but it was a ripple lost in a fast-moving stream of thoughts and fears. She ran up beside him.

'You'll get a message to your dad for me, won't you?' he said. 'And my aunt and uncle. Let them know I won't be home tonight. There's one train that goes out to Kegonsa in the afternoon and one that runs back in the morning. It's, what, a five-hour trip each way?' Elwyn was calculating out loud. The bells atop the city hall chimed. 'I can make it, but I need to run. If nothing goes wrong, I should be back tomorrow afternoon.'

'Elwyn!' she said. 'Stop.' He turned towards her. Her eyes were earnest. 'Listen. The trial's in a couple of days. If your friend's father is innocent, he needs our help.'

Elwyn's stomach started to feel heavy, like he had swallowed a stone. Visions of the protest flooded his mind, the familiarity of the voices, the sounds. Sweat pooled on his temples. 'Whim must be worried. I need to talk to her. I can't just let her go through all this alone.'

'If her father's been coerced into confessing to something he hasn't done, you need to do what you can to be sure wrongs are righted,' Hestia said. 'You need to find him a good lawyer. You need to prepare for the trial and speak for him. That's the way your friend needs you most.'

'I don't know how to find him a good lawyer. I don't know anything. All I know is that my friend is in trouble and I need to be with her.'

'No one's asking you to do it alone. I can help you, but not if you are going to be foolish and rash.' Hestia's face was very serious. 'This isn't about you, Elwyn. This is about protecting the life of an innocent man,' Hestia said. 'Go back to your friend when you have something more to offer than your condolences.'

# CHAPTER 24

# *Campaign*

WHEN ELWYN WAS LITTLE, he sometimes asked Whim what had happened to her mother. Once he asked if her mother was an angel. She said no.

'Don't you believe in angels?' he had said. And she said she only believed in one kind of angel – not angels of people, but angels of places. She said you could almost see them sometimes, hovering just above the earth. And they were very beautiful, so beautiful it could scare you if you let it, much more than any ghost could. 'What are they made of?' Elwyn had asked.

'I don't know. Different things. Space, mostly. But I think the angels here are also made of dew.'

The dew was heavy that next morning. It soaked into the ground, soaked the rooftops and soaked Elwyn's trouser legs as he walked once again to the Rhoad house. The dew was as heavy as the air – the day would be a stifling one, but Elwyn refused to be slowed. He could feel his life starting to unravel around him. Aelred in jail, missing letters – these were just the first frayed edges. He walked quickly, a list in his pocket of the things he needed to talk to Rhoad about, and the things to talk to Hestia about. But when he arrived, Rhoad was not in his office. The house was unusually active, the old housekeeper hobbling back and forth.

'Rhoads are in the sitting room,' she said, in the same sharp voice she had first used with Elwyn. She was walking a box of silver out of the parlour. 'You're to go there right away, not that I see what use you are to them.'

Glass glinted in the morning light. Rhoad, his wife and daughter were well washed and bright at first glance. More closely, beneath her shining hairdo, Letitia wore her usual vague boredom. Hestia didn't look tired, but she looked serious. The events of the day before were evident on her face as she looked at Elwyn. She seemed eager to speak to him. Only Rhoad had a true brightness to his countenance.

'Elwyn, take a seat,' Rhoad said, not looking up as he poured himself a cup of coffee from the silver pot. 'I have good news.' Elwyn sat, looking at Hestia. Her mouth was in a tight line, holding back the things she couldn't say. 'It seems our polls are on the rise again. The dialogue we've cultivated about progress has been a mixed bag, but seeing a Forester in a service role has been very comforting to people, especially the rural population. Emphasising that more Foresters in our society would mean an on-demand workforce seems to be a winning strategy, especially since farmers don't have enough labour during the harvest season.'

'How do the Foresters like that message?' Hestia said, unable to restrain herself.

'I've said it before: politics is storytelling, Hestia,' Rhoad said. 'I don't need to have a story for the Foresters because the Foresters don't participate much in elections. The farmers, though, count for a lot when it comes to votes. They are normally staunchly conservative. If we get half of them, this election will be ours. That is what I'm going to tell you about. We are going on a campaign tour.'

'Tour?' Elwyn said. 'When?'

'Tonight. I don't believe in dallying. We'll travel by train to St Louis, then by car up through the Hill Country to the Messipi headwaters and back around. A month-long tour. My campaign advisor will be here in an hour to go over the details. You know Walter.'

Elwyn's mouth went dry. These words would have once thrilled him – travel, a car, being escorted around the country by wealthy, beautiful people. But when he looked into the future, all he could see was Aelred's face. All he could hear was the bitterness in Aelred's voice.

'Mr Rhoad. I need to talk to you. I'm. . . I'm not sure if the schedule will work for me,' Elwyn said.

'Of course it will work,' Rhoad said, matter-of-factly. 'This is a campaign and you are assisting me. It is your job. Your uncle has already been informed. He's an easy man to sway. He will comply.'

Elwyn looked at Hestia again, but she said nothing. Her mouth went tighter.

'It's not just my uncle. There's something else. I need your help. It's my friend—' he began.

'Oh, yes, I know all about you and my daughter visiting your "friend" yesterday. I know you're troubled by this man's situation, but I can promise you that is even more reason to distance yourself. He is being charged for a crime, and will receive a trial as all people accused do. Involving yourself will not help him, and it will certainly harm you,' Rhoad said.

'But Mr Rhoad, what could harm me more than ignoring my conscience? I only need to stay behind for a few days, until the trial is over. Then I'll come. It won't make much difference.'

'Of course it will make a difference. Don't you understand?' Rhoad said. 'It's imperative that you not be seen with this man. My future depends on it, not to mention your own. You think these farmers we are counting on want to see pictures of you next to a man they see as the manifestation of all their fears? No. They want to see you out in the fields looking healthy and helpful. That may sound degrading but, make no mistake, politics *is* degrading.'

'I can't go,' Elwyn said.

'This tour is built around you, around the message your presence sends,' Rhoad said. 'The men at the courthouse have already had to be paid – and not cheaply – to forget the two of you visiting the jail yesterday. We won't have any more missteps. This campaign is about the future of this country. It is of the utmost importance. You, Elwyn, will be coming on this tour.'

Elwyn said nothing more. Hestia was still quiet. Walter came in, and told them all about the details of the trip: itineraries, fundraising functions, speeches, accommodation. They'd be staying at inns and travelling by car – things Elwyn had so often dreamed of doing. And Elwyn saw that the logic was sound. Aelred said he didn't want his assistance. Rhoad said Elwyn's interference would help no one. And Rhoad's campaign might change things for Foresters.

But logic only went so far; how could Elwyn trust a man who put progress before people? Whim's father might be facing his death. Elwyn couldn't leave him behind.

'I'm having your things sent for,' Rhoad said. 'If your aunt and uncle wish to say goodbye in person before we leave, I've sent word that they are welcome to come here and do so. Otherwise, the day will be spent in preparation.'

'Sir, it's breakfast time,' the housekeeper said at the door.

'Excellent,' Rhoad said. 'We'll continue this in the breakfast parlour. Walter will discuss the rest of the details with us as we eat. We have no time to waste.'

But as everyone left the sitting room, Hestia pulled Elwyn down a side hallway and began to run. They ran through the kitchen and out the servants' door, and Hestia kept on running. Elwyn did not fall behind.

# CHAPTER 25

# *Doubt*

BEHIND THE RHOAD HOUSE, away from town and the river, was a wide, pretty stable. It was situated above the acres of rolling pasture where horses grazed. They were raised not for transport or pleasure, but for the prestige of breeding horses that others coveted. It was Letitia's pet project; Rhoad himself didn't care for the animals. They belonged in the past. And like a vision of the past, they gleamed in the dewy grass, not turning their heads as Hestia and Elwyn ran towards the stable. Only the goat grazing among them sprang happily to the fence.

'Not now, Willoughby,' Hestia said, running inside the stable and down the rows of sweet-smelling doors. At the far corner, they climbed up the ladder that took them to the hayloft. It was dark there. The hot air was thick with the smell of straw dust and the only light came in through cracks in the wood and a small window that looked out over the pastures and valley and the road from the east. They sat down on the hay, panting from the run and the heat.

'We had to get out of there,' Hestia said. 'They'll have their eye on us until we get to the campaign train. We need to think up a plan.'

'Do you think we should be here? They're going to come looking for us.'

'Oh, let them. What can they do? They need our cooperation on this tour, especially yours.' Hestia paused, wiping sweat from her brow. Even in the dark, the air was hot and heavy. She chuckled bitterly. 'A campaign tour. Announced the day after we talk to your friend in jail. Well played.'

'We could go now, run down to the jailhouse and see if we can talk to Aelred again.'

'Haven't you learned anything? Being bold and impulsive doesn't solve things like this, Elwyn. Don't you see? We have to think bigger, more long-term. We have to think like my father.'

'I never want to think like him. Even if I could have everything he had.'

'It's all dirty money, anyway.'

'Only rich people call money dirty,' Elwyn said.

'I am serious, Elwyn. Sometimes I think there is something wrong with the money we have. Like it's cursed. Think about what my father had to do to get it. And what the people had to do to get it before him. And what the people before them had to do and the people before them. The gold itself was dug up in mines from the earth. How many animals' homes were destroyed getting down to that gold? How many people were displaced or hurt or slaughtered? Pain and injustice doesn't disappear from the world.'

Through the light slanting from the window, the dust was visible, hanging in the air like thousands of gnats.

'We'll be cooperative today. Or seem to be. Then on the campaign train, we'll get off at the first stop,' Hestia said. 'My mother will be in the bar car and my father always works on trains. They won't notice we're gone until the next morning when we get to St Louis. We can walk back here, find a lawyer, do what we can for that man in jail. And then we need to figure out why he is there. What systems put him there. This is just the beginning.'

Elwyn turned to the little window and looked out. But now, beyond the horses and Willoughby, way down at the end of the east road, Elwyn saw something strange.

'What's that?' he asked. It looked like there were people approaching in the distance on the east road – many of them, all on foot. 'Is there a circus or something coming into town?'

'It doesn't look like a circus. It looks like. . .' Hestia squinted into the distance. 'It looks like Foresters.' She seemed to have some hunch, some understanding of what was going on, and she jumped down from the hay and began climbing down the ladder. 'Come on,' she said to Elwyn.

He looked out the window and saw that Hestia was right, they were Foresters. A queer feeling filled Elwyn's stomach, a memory of the scent of woodsmoke. The two of them went out of the stable, then through the pasture,

Willoughby at their heels, to the east road. The morning sun shone in their eyes. They didn't run, but walked in long strides, like they knew they were walking towards their fate.

# CHAPTER 26

# *Change*

ELWYN AND HESTIA looked straight ahead, walking steadily, not talking. Willoughby traipsed behind. He didn't chew on Elwyn's clothes now – his new, smart things were less appealing. As they neared, they could make out individuals from out of the mass. Someone caught Elwyn's eye. It was just a glimpse of a person in the distance, there at the front of the crowd. It was the way her hair lay. A way of moving. The shock that moved through him was like lightning. It shot through his body, through his mind and ears.

'Whim. It's Whim,' Elwyn said. Hestia turned to him, confused, but Elwyn hardly noticed. He left Hestia's side and ran ahead with a speed he never had before. Wind pushed against him; crickets along the roadside jumped out of his way like tiny parting waves.

It was not a short run, but Elwyn didn't tire. His eyes began to tear. But as he got closer, Elwyn's gait slowed. Whim looked different. She was at the front of the crowd. The very front. And now and again she turned around to face the people, to call out some message or to lead them in chanting. Her cheeks were flushed, glowing with energy.

Whim was so consumed by what she was doing that she didn't see Elwyn until he was right there beside her. When she saw him, she didn't say his name. She looked at him. And if Elwyn felt Whim could see through him before, he felt it all the more now. But her eyes were not so merciful. There was power there, power Elwyn could sense immediately, even before he realised that it was her that the people were following. And, maybe for the first time, Elwyn could read Whim, too. He could see that she knew about her father, and that she had come there to free him.

The two of them stared at each other until Elwyn spoke. 'I'm coming with you.'

Hestia then arrived at Elwyn's side. 'What's going on?' she said, catching her breath with her hands on her knees. Whim was quiet for a moment, her face unreadable. The three of them had stopped, but the crowd had a life of its own, set on a course like a river. It moved around them, parting as if for stones. The people's faces were full of light. 'Is this another protest? A larger one?' Elwyn and Whim were still looking at each other. 'You must be Whim Moone,' Hestia said, eyeing Whim more carefully. 'Daughter of Aelred Moone. Elwyn told me you're like a sister to him.'

'I'm not his sister,' Whim said, glancing at Hestia only briefly. 'Elwyn. I didn't follow you when you came to Liberty, and there is no reason for you to follow me now,' she said.

'Follow you where?' Hestia said.

'I am going to take my father back home where he belongs.'

'Just like that?' Hestia said.

'No. We're not foolish. We've read the Liberty papers. They've talked about the new safety protocol for violent protests. Everyone is supposed to go into their houses, lock the doors and stay there. It will just be us and the militia and the jail's guards. We are unarmed, but we are many, and we aren't afraid.'

'Even if you get him out of jail, then what?' Hestia said. 'Wouldn't it be better for him to be found innocent by trial? I'm happy to see another protest, but there is a system here, and if you want to change it, you have to change it from the inside.'

'"Change it from the inside"?' Whim said. 'That's a lot easier when you are not a person living out in the woods. We Foresters have never been on the inside, nor do we want to be. You know who I am? Well, I know who you are, Hestia Rhoad, and I know about your father. He talks about inclusion, but his words are deceiving. Any inclusion is not for our sake, but for the wallets of men like him. We may live in the margins, but at least in these margins we are free. And we have come together to free my father and defend our land according to our own ways, not yours.'

'Defend our land?' Elwyn said. 'Whim, what are you talking about?'

Hestia was looking at Whim cautiously, but Whim was no longer paying Hestia any mind. She only studied Elwyn's face and then said, 'Rhoad bought Badfish Creek, Elwyn. All the land around it for miles. We've been told to leave.'

'Bought it? No one can buy a town,' Elwyn said.

'He's building mines. Sand mines. Sand for plate glass that will be used in the cities he wants to build when he opens up the Collective to trade. The genius of it is that he'll build the plant right there, too. Right where Badfish Creek is. And the people who have been displaced will come back and work in the mines and the factory. Any money he pays out for relocation will be earned back a thousandfold in the cheap labour he'll wring from us. That's what happened in Freetown down in the south.'

'Freetown? I don't know what you're talking about, Whim,' Elwyn said. Hestia's face had gone red and her eyes darkened.

At that moment, noise rippled through the crowd around them, and they turned. The militiamen were coming over the hill from Liberty. Some were on horseback, but most were on foot. Whim's eyes went to them, then returned to Elwyn.

'Why don't you go home, Elwyn. To your aunt's house, where you belong.' She looked once more at her old friend, then turned to the masses of people around her and jogged up to the front of the crowd. As she did, Whim began to sing an old Forester song, back from the

**189**

days of the Second War. Elwyn had forgotten what a clear voice she had.

> *Through the wood among the reeds,*
> *We who wrought the lives we please. . .*

Others joined in, and Whim's voice was lost to Elwyn. He ran after her, but the crowd made it impossible to reach her. The voices bounced off the sun-dappled hills.

'Elwyn! I knew you'd join us,' said a familiar voice from the crowd. It was Caradoc Alfin. Elwyn had been so focused on Whim, he hadn't noticed anyone else. Looking around now, many of the people were familiar; some of them came in from deep in the woods to shop at Wilder's store and pick up their mail. Others from Badfish Creek came into focus, too. People Elwyn had known since childhood, their faces nearly as transformed as Whim's. Caradoc slapped Elwyn on the back. 'We aren't going to let them take what's ours, are we? We will defend our people, defend our land.'

'Defend our land,' Elwyn repeated, like a child mimics the words of the people around them.

'Other people doubted you, said you had forgotten us. Your mam asked that none of us speak to you because she didn't want you giving up your safety. But I knew it wouldn't do any good. I knew you'd find out what was going on. Like Whim says, the land has a will, you know, the land speaks.'

Elwyn didn't know what to say. He heard what his friends said, he saw the purpose in their steps, he felt their energy around him. He felt it pulsing in his own veins. The protesters drew closer to town, step by step, verse by verse of the old song. Elwyn ran ahead towards Whim, his mind too busy to sing. When he reached her side he walked along with her, matching her stride. He didn't say anything, but kept looking over at her, as if what he needed to understand might be hidden somewhere in her face. But she looked straight ahead. West. Chin lifted to the sun.

Ahead on the road, horses trotted towards them with militiamen darkly dressed. A few were drawing near, while a few dozen more hung back like clouds in the sky. Hestia had joined them at the front of the crowd, followed by Willoughby, who was excited by the people and horses.

'Whim, what happened back at home? Where's Mam? Where are my brothers and sisters?' Elwyn said.

'We've been kicked off our land, Elwyn. People who aren't prepared to fight for it are leaving.'

'What do you mean, they're leaving?'

'They've left. Your family has left. The Elises have left. Janie Wilder has left – March is dead.'

'March is dead?'

'Terrible things have happened to us, Elwyn. And just because you weren't there to see it doesn't mean it wasn't as real.' Elwyn felt like he had taken a hit. Like he had fallen from some place high. He didn't know what to say, but Hestia stepped in first.

'And you say my father is responsible?' Hestia asked. 'He should be held accountable for what he has done. I won't let him get away with this.'

Whim looked at Hestia a bit longer, then as they walked, her eyes went to something behind her, up in the direction of Hestia's house. Hestia and Elwyn both turned. Rhoad himself was striding down the hill. A couple of men followed him, men Elwyn recognised as hired guards.

'Whim. What's the plan?' Elwyn said. She didn't answer. Her eyes were glued to Rhoad, but she didn't alter her course. They couldn't hear Rhoad above the roar of the crowd, but they could see him nod in their direction, and the men following him slipped through the crowd towards Elwyn and Hestia.

'Sorry, Miss Rhoad. I'm under orders to get you to safety. It's for your own protection,' one of the men said. Hestia tried to fight him off, but he held her. Few of the protesters saw this, being so focused on their goal, their forward momentum. But those who did see didn't help her, not even Whim. Elwyn lunged at the man, but the other guard grabbed him roughly and without apology. Caradoc Alfin jumped in to help Elwyn free himself. By the time he did, Hestia was being dragged away.

Elwyn rushed through the protesters towards her. He could see that the militiamen on horses were nearing the demonstrators. People started to pick up rocks and throw them at the horses' feet. The horses reared up a little, but the militiamen weren't discouraged. One of them began to laugh, and Elwyn saw that his face was familiar. The goat keeper. The one who had followed Elwyn to the Blackwell house, who had fallen unconscious on the floor.

The man saw Elwyn, too. And he turned his horse away from the crowd and to Elwyn, who was running towards the house after Hestia.

'Let's have a bit of fun,' the man said to no one in particular, and he grabbed Elwyn by one of his arms, dragging him through the grass. Elwyn was dangerously close to the horse's feet, but could do nothing to free or right himself. It was like being pulled down in the current of a river. The horse trotted and Elwyn's arm screamed, pulled at its socket.

Even as this all was happening, Elwyn could hardly believe it was real. It passed like a painful dream. He was Elwyn Bramble. Son of Mirth. Son of Badfish Creek. The boy destined for greatness. He was being dragged through Liberty behind a horse. Whim was leading a march to rescue her father from jail. Badfish Creek was in danger. None of it hung together. It was like a bizarre dream, one that Elwyn couldn't wake from.

The man didn't take Elwyn back to the house, but led him behind the stable. Elwyn tried to run, but his legs were weak and bruised. The goat man grabbed him.

'Don't worry. I've got orders to take you back to the house,' he said. 'The Rhoads are going on tour, and we aren't supposed to let any harm come to their precious Forester pet. We wouldn't want the tree trash to look bad in his fancy pictures. But then again. . .' He lifted his knee violently, planting it in Elwyn's spine, and Elwyn fell to the ground. 'I've been waiting for this a long time, tree trash,' the man said, again smelling of alcohol. 'Done up so fine. Making such important friends.' He kicked Elwyn in the head, and that was the last thing Elwyn could remember.

# CHAPTER 27

# *Victors*

THERE IS AN UNDERSTANDING somewhere in the human spirit that the weak can come together to defeat the strong. In the First War, Americans rose up against the King and demanded their own country. In the Second War, slaves rose up against their masters and demanded their freedom. These were histories embedded in the world Whim grew up in, embedded in her bones. These were the stories she was told, the songs she had sung. She believed the unity of her people was more powerful than weapons and money. Of course she did, or why would she have done the things she had done?

But there was still a part of her that didn't think what she hoped for was possible. Part of her had feared what she was leading people into: failure, maybe. Even death. But when the militia rushed at them with their guns and horses, these doubts were crowded out of her mind. It was like there was not only a wind at her back, but a storm.

And what happened seemed like a miracle to Whim. Guns were fired, but mostly they missed. Horses ran at the crowd, but were frightened back. Of the hundreds of protesters Whim led, only a dozen were trampled or shot, and none of these injuries were fatal. The Foresters' numbers outweighed the militia's weapons, and Whim could see as they closed in on the men that they were afraid. They tied the militia to trees and set the horses free, and then they walked into the silent, shuttered town.

Whim could feel the eyes of the people of Liberty on them. No one left their homes, and whether it was because they were afraid or obedient to safety procedures, Whim didn't know. But she believed that the things she had planned came to pass. She believed that through shutters and blinds they were watching, and they saw them as people. It felt almost like magic to Whim. She knew this was the way the world was built; it was made not for the greedy few, but for the just. Yet it still surprised her that together a group of Foresters could walk the streets, force their way into a jail, and not be afraid.

The courthouse was ringed with several guards. Whim's heart was in her throat. Her father was just behind them, behind the walls. The guards carried metal clubs, and Whim locked eyes with one of them, the largest and most menacing.

The man raised his club, but before Whim could speak, he had turned and hit the guard next to him with it, then the next one.

'For justice! For Aelred!' the man called out. Whim wished she could get a better look at the man who had been a friend to her father and delivered her letters, but there was no time. The protesters swarmed the jail like bees swarm a hive. It was a tiny place, so much smaller than she had imagined, and it was soon spilling over with bodies. Whim was the one who found the stairs, who first went down them. She was the first one to see her father, and the first one her father saw. His face was yellow with old bruises and purple with new ones. But when he looked up at her, his face was so proud.

'Little Whim,' he said.

'Quick, let's get down this door,' Whim said, and the people produced a metal desk-chair, which they rammed at the door until it gave way. Aelred hugged his daughter, his face teary and wet, and together they all shouted and sang through the streets. They left the town as though they had conquered it. But just as they reached the edge of the little city, they heard whistles and the sound of more horse hooves.

'Run!' Aelred shouted, and the protesters fled into fields of high corn.

They moved quietly through the farmland and were cautious and quick, but not afraid. They felt they had already done the impossible and could do impossible things yet. The walked all through the day until they reached the forest, and under the cover of the oaks, they made camp. People talked around the fire, about what they had seen that day and what they had done. Whim and her father sat off to the side, soaking in the victorious atmosphere around them as they bathed in the day's heat, the flying insects, the last fireflies.

'You've succeeded where I've failed, little Whim. A father has never been more proud of his daughter.'

But Whim, despite the intoxicating feeling of victory and the joy of reunion, had one spot in her mind that was dim, one thing that disturbed her.

'I saw Elwyn,' she said. 'He came as we were walking into Liberty, he and Hestia Rhoad. Rhoad sent people after them. He was dragged behind a horse.' The words disgusted her as she said them – they were tough, like meat freshly killed and cut. 'Other people tried to stop it. But I didn't do anything. I just let them drag him away.'

Even as she spoke, she expected her father to say that she had done right, that she was a bird and he was a badger, that he had made his choice. Instead, her father put his hand gently to her face, brushed away the hair, sweaty from the heat and movement of the day, that had fallen over her eyes.

'Your compassion is the well of your strength. Be more careful not to lose it.'

That night the protesters slept hard and well. People took turns keeping watch. Whim was sitting up, staring at the stars, when she heard a rustle from the bushes. She straightened herself, listening closely and preparing to sound the alarm, when she heard a familiar voice.

'Enid, I'm telling you, I saw campfire smoke coming from right around here.'

'Great. Campfire smoke. It could be bandits, you know. We could have done all this work to pluck up our courage and become heroic and all that nonsense, only to be robbed and killed.'

'We don't have anything anyone wants to steal.'

'Enid? Neste?' Whim called.

'See. I was right.'

'Oh, shut up. Whim! Where are you?'

When Enid and Neste saw Whim, they dropped the packs they carried and the three of them wrapped each other in an embrace.

'We're so glad you're okay,' Neste said.

'You are all on your way back to Badfish Creek?' Enid said. 'How did it go? Did you see Elwyn? Did you get your father?'

'We figured we'd already missed our chance to help free Aelred, but we can still do our part protecting our homeland,' Neste said. 'Mam didn't want to let us go, and, to tell the truth, we were a bit nervous, too. But we just kept thinking about you, and what you would do in our shoes.'

'You make the rest of us look cowardly, Whim Moone, and I won't stand for it,' Enid said.

The three of them sat together, Whim telling Enid and Neste about the march through Liberty and the plans for the following days. Then, when relieved of guard duties, the girls unfurled their bed rolls and fell into a brief, deep sleep.

Before the protesters marched on in the morning, they erased traces of the night's camp and gathered together.

'We are children of survivors: survivors of war, survivors of slavery, survivors of empire. They may tell us to bend, but we will not bend. They may try to buy us, but we will not be bought. Our way of life is our inheritance, and the strength of those who have gone before us runs through our veins. We will not be moved.' Aelred spoke and people murmured in agreement. Their plan was to assemble even more people, spread word along the creeks and rivers from the Messipi to the Laurentian Lakes and beyond.

The details were discussed as they marched along, far from the main road. They knew they could navigate the woods with an ease unmatched by those who hadn't spent generations there. This was one of their advantages. So though they kept alert, and listened for people pursuing them, the protesters went with confidence. They slept as well the second night as they did the first, with the knowledge that home was near, that what was precious was close at hand.

The final miles to Badfish Creek were walked singing loudly, announcing their victory. It was early morning, and the sky was grey with clouds. But something was not quite right. Whim couldn't place it, but it was something about the light and the shape of the horizon to the south and east. As they neared the road, tyre tracks marred the path they walked. The soil below them was dense like skin below a scar. Plants and branches on either side of the road were torn. One by one, voices dropped out of the song. Other sounds could be heard. The caws of jays and crows, the twittering of robins. Squirrels were yelling.

Then they heard the sound of a tree falling. The sound of saws working. The sound of shovels, of an engine. Whim's heart was in her throat, and her knees, which to this point felt strong despite full days of walking, now felt weak. She looked at her father. He was pale, and Neste and Enid looked confused. Aelred reached out his hand for hers and she took it.

The first thing Whim saw was the space where the Bramble house had been. It was now an empty place, a pile of rubble beside it. There was a stack of several trees that had been felled and piled, and two men were working there, sawing down branches. Holes where trunks had been pulled from the ground dotted the forest floor, and all around them soil was turned over – soil that hadn't been turned for centuries, that was layered with the humus of leaves, the coming and going of pigeons, that told the story of the land like tree rings.

The smell of exhaust was still in the air, and in the distance Whim could see one of the large trucks like the one she had seen that first day. It had a chain behind it and was struggling to pull old roots from the ground. There was a yell and a crack as another tree fell, shaking the ground below them and filling Whim's ears. The protesters began to step out onto the freshly turned soil, its smell sickeningly sweet below their feet, soft as flesh. Bits of cups and bowls cracked under them and one of the newspaper clippings from Enid and Neste's room blew by. Neste picked it up.

'Hey!' the man cutting back the stack of trees shouted. He waved to the man driving, and he turned the truck off. 'You're trespassing,' the man said, walking towards them. 'We've been ordered to keep out any trespassers.' He slung the axe he wielded over his shoulder. Behind him, Whim could see the other men walking towards them, each with their axe, their saw, their heavy shovel.

'We aren't leaving,' Whim said loudly. 'There are hundreds of us.'

The man who was driving the truck opened the back and pulled out a rifle, which he loaded as he walked towards them, too. 'Are these the rebels we're supposed to be on the lookout for?' he asked.

'It doesn't matter,' the first man said. 'Trespassers are trespassers. These Foresters need to be taught who's in charge out here.' And as the man with the rifle raised it, Whim did something she didn't know she had the courage to do. She let go of her father's hand and ran towards the man, ran with all the strength left in her legs.

## CHAPTER 28

# *The First Blow*

SHE EXPECTED THE MAN to change the aim of the gun towards herself, and perhaps he did. Her mind was too uniformly focused on her task to really see the world that blurred around her. She ran low and grabbed the man around the waist, knocking him to the ground as the gun went off. There was a swell of sound from the crowd behind her, the sound of courage, of feet moving forward on the soil. Whim took the gun and climbed to her feet, but the man reached up and grabbed the middle of the barrel, trying to pull it from her.

Then Whim heard a sound she had never heard before. It was the crack of a shovel coming down on a skull. The sound shook Whim's bones, and as she looked towards the sound, she lost her grip. There was a scream. In the second Whim's eyes scanned the crowd, the man had jabbed the stock end of the rifle into Whim's stomach and was walking away. The pain was so great, Whim doubled over. The noise of fighting rose around her.

'You forest trash need to know your place,' the man said, now turning the gun to point it at Whim. She willed her body to fight back, but in that moment, she couldn't move. Before the trigger could be pulled, her father ran at the man, one of the broken bottles from the ground in his hand. He thrust the bottle into the man's neck. There was blood, there was so much blood. Whim had heard stories of Forester men who lost their limbs and lives on Hill farm machinery, but she had never pictured as much blood as she saw in that moment, bubbling out, pooling in the dirt.

Aelred turned white and dropped to his knees where the man had fallen. Around them were yells and the thuds of shovels, of axes. Whim kept looking up, trying to see if everyone was all right. But the world was out of focus. All Whim really saw was her father beside her, the horror in his face as he took off his own shirt and tried to stop the bleeding. She couldn't see the man with the heavy stick until it was too late. He came up behind her father. Hit him over the head. Another thud. It took only seconds. Less than seconds.

'No!' Whim cried.

'Whim. My little Whim,' he said. Then the stick crashed down over her own head. One moment her eyes were filled with her father on the ground, another man's blood soaking his clothes. The next moment everything went black.

When Whim Moone woke, her father was still there. He was crumpled. Still blood-soaked. Still handsome. He and the man whose head he held were both dead.

# CHAPTER 29

# Insects and Empire

WHEN ELWYN WAS FOUR, a tornado came through the forest. His family sheltered in a bank by the creek, below a tangle of roots. And when the storm passed, they all came up into a forest covered with debris. One house, just one, had been damaged. The Colliers'. It had been one of the old homes built around a tree, and the tree had been uprooted. But the house, instead of being smashed, was sitting neatly beside the topmost branches. Its roof had been pulled off and put back on upside down, as if by hands.

The world had seemed all wrong then. Confusing and surreal, like it looks in a dream. Elwyn had been a young child. Everything was tall and saturated and twisted in the purple post-storm light. That was the way the world seemed to Elwyn when he woke in his room at the Blackwell house. The world was upside down, tossed.

Whim came into his foggy mind. A bright, glowing vision. All these months, Elwyn had been focused on his goals, of making something of himself. He had been so proud. Proud of his own cleverness, his pluck. In mere months, Elwyn had gone from being a Forester with three sets of clothes, to the assistant of one of the richest men in the Collective. Who wouldn't be proud?

But now, from where he lay, dirty on his bed at the Blackwells', it all seemed shabby. For weeks, Aelred had been in the Liberty jail. Badfish Creek had been in trouble. His family had been kicked off their land. People had been struggling for something that mattered.

While Elwyn had been getting his photograph taken and practising speeches, Whim had become this whole other person. The sort of person who stands at the front of a crowd. The sort of person who casts light. It was her light that threw Elwyn's life into such sharp relief. While everything else around him was dim and confused, Elwyn could see one thing clearly. He saw that Whim had done something real. Something of lasting value. And he and everything he was striving for was just a shadow in comparison. Less than a shadow.

'You're awake,' his aunt said as she walked into the room, holding a cold cloth in her hand. She placed it on his forehead, removing the now-warm one that had been there. Looking around, Elwyn saw that there were bowls of water beside him, herbs and compresses. She sat on the stool beside the bed and checked his eyes and his pulse.

'What am I doing here?' Elwyn said.

'The equine manager found you at the Rhoads' stable after the riot. You were badly hurt,' she said with her usual crispness. 'The political tour has been postponed. There will be a speech at some point regarding the riot, and if you are well enough, they've requested your attendance. But I think you'd be a fool to sacrifice your health for someone else.'

None of this seemed important to Elwyn in that moment. 'Hestia. Is Hestia okay? And what happened to the protesters? Is the trial still going forward?' Elwyn said, sitting up urgently, only to find his head swimming and his back aching. He winced and lay back. Piety adjusted things for him and answered in her usual methodical way.

'All the Rhoads are safe. For such a large demonstration, the serious injuries have been few. Only the jail's guards were seriously hurt, and that wasn't due to the protesters – they say that one of the guards went insane and turned on the others. All in all, it was a rousing success for safety policy and procedure. Your uncle will be thrilled,' she said with an unpleasant smile. 'As for the trial, it seems the aim of this demonstration was to free the man from jail, and in that they have succeeded, though what hope they can have of keeping him out of court in the long term, I don't know. It's not my business.'

Elwyn's head was still spinning. The details blurred. He didn't know what the time was; he wasn't even sure of the day. He rolled over onto his side and tried to sit up, wincing. He stood on aching legs and made his way over to his desk, hunched like an old man. He opened the drawer, each movement aching and difficult, and pulled out his wallet.

'What are you doing?' Piety asked.

'What time is it?' Elwyn said. 'I need to catch a train. . .' But he stopped speaking. He had opened his wallet and found it empty. His mind was so addled, at first he thought he wasn't seeing right. He clumsily dug his fingers into the corners of the leather. 'Someone's stolen. . .' he began, but couldn't finish. His head was swimming and he had to lower himself to the ground.

'Your money is safe,' Piety said.

Elwyn looked up at his aunt. 'Safe?'

'I know you think I'm without ideals or beliefs, but I'm not an unprincipled person. I still believe in honesty. Being true to oneself, true to one's word. Long ago, I promised your mother that if I ever took you in, I would keep you safe. That is what I said, and so that is what I have done. No more, no less.'

'. . .my letters. . .' Elwyn said, holding his stomach and looking up at his aunt once again.

'I was afraid you might do something rash. They were set aside for your safety. Just look at you now.' Elwyn couldn't speak, betrayal and nausea were so strong in his stomach. 'Believe me, it wasn't easy for me to stomach falling into the role of censor. I believe in openness in discourse. But I am bound to my word.'

'*Your* word. *You* are bound,' Elwyn said from where he sat on the ground, head resting against the cool wood of the desk. He shifted his body, wincing, then sighed. 'I thought you and I were different. You liked to say no to the world, and I liked to say yes. But we're actually the same. It's all about us, isn't it? All about my dreams. All about your doubts, your honour. We can't see anything else. We can't see anyone but ourselves, and what's right in front of us,' Elwyn snorted.

There was the bitter taste of bile in Elwyn's mouth, the taste of self-disgust. His aunt was quiet as Elwyn used the desk to raise himself up to standing. With effort, he straightened his back, lifted his chest and chin. Stiffly he walked out of his room, down the clock-laden hall, into the foyer and out of the front door. Stiffly, painfully, he walked the familiar way to the Rhoad house. Elwyn didn't have to think; his feet knew the path well. The sky was overcast. Doors and windows were closed and shuttered. The Rhoad house, like the town below it, was very quiet. Elwyn went to the back door, but the housekeeper wasn't there, and nor was the cook.

'Hestia?' Elwyn called out as he entered the dining room, then the main hall. His ribs hurt as he spoke. A ripple of worry ran down his legs, and again his stomach turned. But then he heard a sound from Rhoad's private office.

The door was ajar. And in the middle of it was Hestia. Papers scattered and flew around her as she rifled through a box of receipts, the dull light of a grey day casting a strange tone over the scene.

When she heard Elwyn's footsteps, Hestia looked up with a directness and fierceness unusual even for her.

'Do you believe it? What your friend said about my father seizing land?' Hestia challenged.

'I believe everything Whim says,' Elwyn said, his heart in his throat as he spoke.

'I believe her, too,' Hestia said, turning back to the papers. She handed Elwyn a stack of messy forms and maps. As she did, her eyes scanned his battered appearance. 'Are you okay?' she asked gravely.

'I'm okay. I came here because I'm going home,' Elwyn said. 'I want you to come with me.'

'Elwyn, look at the papers,' she said.

'What are they?' Elwyn said, scanning words of a contract.

'It's everything. Everything I found so far anyway. Letters from local magistrates requesting financial rewards for their cooperation. Receipts for relocation funds. Plans for the mine. Contracts with demolition workers. A glass-factory floor plan. My father illegally used a loophole to seize the land. He said the Foresters' being there was dangerous to "the progress of the Collective". He'd done it before, too, and I don't know how he's gotten away with it. It would never hold up in court. Meanwhile, he's putting a sand mine where your town was. He has contracts with builders all over the Collective for glass, beginning production at the start of next year. And look. He has prospective overseas contracts, too, contingent on his Chancellorship and the Collective opening up to trade. The profit margins selling abroad are huge. Forester labour is so cheap.' Elwyn read as Hestia explained, rubbing his shoulder where it ached. 'It's all here. Written in business terms, as if people were just any other resource. The relocation funds are a tiny fraction of the expense. They intentionally made the funds just large enough to tempt very poor people, but still not enough to get them off on the right foot. They want people to come back. To come back and work in the mines.'

Elwyn looked up at her. The reality of it sank in through his skin.

'They're going to tear down your hometown, Elwyn. There will be nothing left. Less than nothing. A hole in the ground.'

Then a sound echoed through the quiet house. Hestia and Elwyn froze. The front door opened and slammed shut.

'Well, that was a waste of time.' Rhoad's voice echoed through the house, uncharacteristically erratic.

'He was at a meeting at the city hall about security and enforcement,' Hestia whispered, quietly gathering papers. 'I didn't expect them home so early.'

'That insufferable Blackwell. Thinks the letter of the law is the word of God. I've never in my life heard someone say the words "proper procedure" so often. These people will be nicely situated at some wilderness hideout by the time the "proper procedures" are done to document the crime. I would think he was trying to help them if I hadn't met men in love with bureaucracy before. It's stupidity.'

'I'm getting a drink,' muttered a rattled-sounding Letitia Rhoad.

'Oh no you don't,' Rhoad said. 'People are terrified. You need to be at your best. The radiant, glistening face of the future.'

'And you think I am not terrified? I, a woman born into education, privilege. . . I had to hide in the cellar with the servants! It's an uprising!'

'Uprising!' Rhoad scoffed. 'It's just poor people trying to make themselves feel in control. It will work for a while, and folks will think that things have changed. But things never change, Letitia. Do you hear me? Things never change. Not for them.'

'What do I have to look good for anyway?' Letitia said, tremulous, with the clink of the decanter opening. 'The tour is postponed. The press is focused on the riot. You've sunk our fortune into this campaign, and now that campaign is over.'

'It is NOT OVER,' Rhoad boomed. His voice echoed down the shimmering halls. Elwyn had never heard Rhoad so much as raise his voice, and the effect made the hairs on the back of his neck stand. 'You will put your drink down. Take a bath, calm your nerves. Then you will put on one of your many beautiful dresses. Your hairdresser will come in to do your hair in one of the many becoming ways it is done. And we will go out and speak to the people – you, me, Hestia and Elwyn, if he looks good enough for the camera. I've already started making the calls. There will be photographers. Dozens of photographers. We will flood the papers with our image and with our words. Our faces, *your face*, will be on the front of every newspaper. Then we'll leave on tour, and there will be more pictures, and more words for the papers. We will change the story people are telling. We will change it. We will change everything.'

'But aren't you worried that they'll be back? These people. . . they have no values, nothing to lose. They just want to take from us what we've earned, what our parents and grandparents have earned. . .'

'Take a bath,' Rhoad said more quietly, but not gently. 'Calm your nerves.' And they could hear footsteps going up the stairs, and after those faded, there was the clink of the decanter, the pouring of a drink.

Hestia was moving quickly and quietly, like the fierce hummingbird she had first reminded Elwyn of, and Elwyn tried clumsily to help her, but movement was painful.

'Hide these papers,' Hestia said, nodding to the open window. Elwyn leant out and secured the stack of paper with a rock below the concealing branches of a bush. When he got back in, the room was almost clear and Rhoad's approaching footsteps could be heard in the hall. The footsteps reminded him of Rhoad walking down towards the protesters, and of Hestia being dragged away.

Perhaps Elwyn should have been afraid in that moment. Rhoad was not an innocent man, and Elwyn had more than ever to lose. But anger pulsed in his veins. Elwyn wanted to look Rhoad in the eye. Rhoad: the man Elwyn had admired so intensely. The man who was destroying Elwyn's home.

'Don't say anything,' Hestia said, then the door swung open. Elwyn turned, ready to face Rhoad with his head high. When Rhoad's eyes met Elwyn, they flashed for a moment with something like disgust. Then they returned to their usual evenness.

'What are you doing in my office?' Rhoad said. They didn't answer. Elwyn felt his face growing red with the anger that was growing in him.

For a moment, the room was completely quiet. The three of them stood looking at one another. The only sound was a mosquito that had flown in through the open window. For a moment, that was what Elwyn could hear, that and his own rising pulse. The buzzing of the mosquito grew louder as it neared them, drawn by the smell of human breath and blood in the air.

'Do you know about the First War, Elwyn? The "Revolutionary War", as it was called?' Rhoad spoke into the silence. The mosquito buzzed around his head, but he kept his eyes glued to his daughter and Elwyn. Rhoad raised his arm; the bare skin below rolled-up sleeves was pale.

'I've had an education,' Elwyn said. Hestia was watching her father carefully, the way a cat watches and waits.

'Before there was a Collective, this country was a colony of the Kingdom of Great Britain. Britain was the centre of civilisation, and the strongest military power in the world. It went on to colonise half the world. But these thirteen backwater colonies were able to throw it off. Do you know why?'

'Yes,' Elwyn said, feeling the heat in his own face as he spoke. 'People loved and believed in something and acted on that love.'

'Wrong. It was *Anopheles quadrimaculatus*. The malarial mosquito.' The mosquito had landed on Rhoad's arm and was beginning to swell with blood. 'Such a small, inconsequential thing. A nuisance. But it overthrew an empire. The settlers had developed resistance to diseases that the British had not. A great power fell. A legacy unravelled.'

'Or perhaps it was the British themselves at fault for their fall,' Hestia said, full of animation. 'For planting the seed of slavery and profiting from it. For making false promises to the tribes and kingdoms that already had claim to the land. For being leaders that serve their own interests, not the interests of the powerless.'

'Hush, Hestia, and for once in your life listen!' Rhoad yelled, purpling. He turned back to Elwyn. 'After the British left, the American colonists ran into their own problems. They had plans for a little empire of their own. "Manifest Destiny", they called it. But always the insects had their way of pushing back: disease, blindness, death.' The mosquito on Rhoad's arm was getting larger and larger. Elwyn watched, frozen in rage and transfixed. 'The smallest things can buck a civilisation if you don't attend to them.'

Rhoad's voice trailed off as the mosquito lifted its proboscis. The insect rose to fly, heavy with blood. But Rhoad lifted the arm that the mosquito had bitten, and without looking caught the mosquito in his hand. He held his fist out towards Elwyn. Then opened it. His palm was stained red. But Rhoad's face was now cool and composed. Ready to give a speech. Ready to have his picture taken.

'Understand, Hestia, Elwyn, I'm not a stupid man. I have eyes everywhere. I can protect those who are loyal to me, and I can destroy those who aren't. Consider this a reminder,' Rhoad said. 'You won't be getting another.'

Hestia lifted her chin.

'I will not be threatened,' she said. Her father brushed the mosquito's tiny body from his hand. 'Least of all by my own father.'

'I've rebooked the campaign tour. It will go on as originally planned, almost exactly. But in light of recent events, we'll be delivering a speech here in Liberty tomorrow morning before we go. You and I will both speak, Elwyn. Our speech-writers are already at work on what we will say. It will be a pivotal moment, not just for this campaign, but the country. We will be the face of a hopeful future in these dark times.' Then he looked at Elwyn more deliberately, in a way that surprised him. 'We really are the face of the future, you and I, Elwyn. My daughter is young and headstrong and naturally doubts all I say. But you should know that for me this is not a game. I don't seek prominence or fortune – both those things

I have. I seek leadership because this country is mired in old prejudices, old failures, old habits. And I know how to get us out.'

Hestia scoffed at this, but Elwyn didn't. It seemed possible to him that what Rhoad had said was true; maybe his intentions weren't just self-serving. It made no difference. Intentions never mattered much to Elwyn. As he was led to the parlour, where jumpy-looking speech-writers sat working, he kept thinking about that pile of papers and what it meant for him, what it meant for the Collective. *Think about what it means for the powerful to deceive the people they serve.*

Elwyn knew what he had to do.

# CHAPTER 30

# The Collective

ELWYN SPENT THE DAY with the Rhoads, closely supervised. Again and again they went over the speech Elwyn was to give, memorising it, adjusting the tone. In the afternoon, Elwyn fell asleep on the sofa when he was supposed to be listening to tweaks being made to the campaign trip. The changes didn't matter to Elwyn because he knew he wouldn't be going on that tour. He wasn't even sure he would be alive. His future seemed very tenuous. In those few moments of sleep, Elwyn dreamt the glistening room they worked in collapsed and he had to dig himself out of gilded rubble and broken glass. He woke with a jolt, but no one asked him if he was all right. Afterwards, they had an early dinner and the meal was silent.

Elwyn was led to the same guest room where he had spent the first night with the Rhoads. The room had looked so beautiful to him then, but seeing it again now made him sad. Elwyn missed the sound of his brothers snoring and turning in their sleep. He missed the sound of crickets and the creek. He worried he would never hear them again. The words he was going to say the next day went over and over in his mind as he drifted in and out of uneasy sleep.

'I have them,' Hestia whispered to Elwyn on their way to the car the next morning. That was all they were able to say to one another. They were shunted apart into different doors of the sleek black car. It was only two miles from the Rhoad house to the centre of Liberty – driving such a short distance was an extravagance that would have once thrilled Elwyn. But now he couldn't shake the feeling that they took the car so Rhoad could keep them. Rhoad's gaze, steely as the sky that hovered above them, didn't leave Elwyn.

In the city centre, the stage was set with a podium, and the reporters stood milling around it. The buzz of adrenalin from the protest was still in the air. People were gathered, talking in heightened tones about where they were when the jail was stormed, where they thought the gunman might be, what they thought would happen next.

'Ah! Here he is! Our nephew Elwyn!' Timothy said, his jowls shaking with enthusiasm as he clapped his hands together. Piety hung back, looking at Elwyn with the same sort of reserve he remembered from his first day in Liberty. Boaz was scowling beside her.

'Let's get a family picture,' said one of the photographers as Elwyn and the Blackwells were shuffled together. The camera flashed.

'There's so much national attention now. This could be on the title page of my book,' Timothy said as Boaz was moved next to Elwyn and told to smile.

'I wish you good luck on your tour,' Piety said from the other side. 'I understand you're going directly from here. Someone came by to collect your things.'

Elwyn didn't answer for a moment. He looked past the flash of the camera to the edges of the town square, where armed men on horses watched over the scene.

'I hope you don't think I'm ungrateful,' Elwyn said quietly. 'I'm glad I got to know you. Despite everything. You meant a lot to me when I was young.' The words felt grave, because Elwyn felt they might be some of his last. If nothing else, he felt sure they would be his last to her. 'I don't hold any grudge against you. We can't control what we love or don't love.'

Elwyn saw a change on his aunt's face, but he had little time to consider her.

'Now, smile,' the photographer said. The light of the camera flashed again.

Elwyn was led to his chair onstage, his fingers tingling. Everything looked sharp and saturated. He could feel his heart pumping in his chest. Hestia and her mother were seated behind the podium, hair smoothed, clothes well-pressed. With a wave of applause, Rhoad rose and limped to the podium, beginning the speech Elwyn had heard so many times before.

'Our nation was founded on principles of independence, freedom and, yes, separation. But it was a separation married to bravery. For too long, an epidemic of fear has pillaged this country. We no longer stay apart in order to build up new lives in accordance with our own principles. We separate ourselves because we are afraid of each other, afraid of the world. This fear has turned what was once our freedom into our shackles. This country, which holds all the marks of greatness, is reduced to an afterthought in the world. But not for long. . .'

Rhoad went on about industry, tools of the future unlocking the wealth and hidden potential in the land, hidden potential in us all. Elwyn watched the people as they listened. A hush had fallen over them; they were rapt, attentive. Even Boaz looked up at Rhoad. Elwyn's mouth became dry as the speech neared its end. Soon Rhoad would call him up, and he would have to say what he came there to say.

Applause rang through the crowd when Rhoad finished. The sound rose into the dull sky, full of energy. Rhoad's face was almost luminous. Elwyn had never seen him look that way, like a painting of a ship's captain. When the applause started to die down, Rhoad started Elwyn's introduction. He gestured to him and everyone clapped again. Elwyn's legs felt weak. But he made his way up to the podium and shook Rhoad's hand. The cameras clicked; lights flashed.

For a moment, Elwyn couldn't find the words he had recited to himself so many times the night before – the words that were in the back of his mind while he ate, while he listened, while he read the words speech-writers had written for him. He stood silently, everything turning a bit around him. Rhoad cleared his throat. Elwyn looked at his clear, well-groomed face. Elwyn recalled other faces. The careworn face of his mother. Aelred in jail. Whim marching.

'Cronus Rhoad had humble beginnings, like me,' Elwyn said. His voice seemed to dissipate into the open square. 'He worked his way to success by selling things. By chopping trees from the north and selling them in New Orleans. By using his earnings to build lumber mills, and using those earnings to dig lead mines, and using those earnings to finance this big campaign. He found potential in things around him and exploited it. This is how wealth is created. This is American success and the reason we want him at the helm of the Collective Homesteads.' There was a light applause. Elwyn's speech wasn't as moving as Rhoad's, nor was it meant to be. Elwyn was there to make people comfortable, to show that change wasn't threatening, that it could be pleasant and mundane.

'But that's a story you have all been told already,' Elwyn said. There was a hush when he spoke these honest words. 'There are other stories out there. Ones from down on the underbelly of this country we've all been born into. Most of those stories will never be told, and the ones that are told will probably be forgotten. But I am going to tell mine anyway.' Elwyn nodded to Hestia, who ran behind the stage and returned with a suitcase, which she opened to display the stacks of papers taken from her father's office.

By this point Elwyn had expected to be stopped by Rhoad, but Rhoad seemed frozen in place. By what, Elwyn couldn't contemplate or understand. Perhaps it was a calculated step, or maybe it was just surprise. Elwyn knew he had to keep talking as long as he could, ride his luck as far as it would take him.

'In this stack of papers are deeds of land that belonged to me,' Elwyn said. 'That belonged to hundreds of people like me. The land had shaped us and our lives for hundreds of years, just as your land has shaped all of you. It has been our livelihood and the life's work of generations.' He paused. 'This summer, Cronus Rhoad took this land illegally. Forced us from our homes.'

The cameras clicked furiously. Elwyn's voice felt stronger. 'Cronus Rhoad likes to tell you that he is a man who can see the potential in this country. He says he can use this land to create wealth for us all. But what has he has ever done but exploit things? Exploit people? Rhoad might see himself as a man of vision, but he's really just another person who builds things to suit himself without worrying about the cost to others. Today it's my people. Tomorrow it could be anyone.' The crowd murmured. Elwyn turned to glance at Rhoad. The man was just sitting in his place, purple-faced.

'Greed didn't begin with Rhoad, and it won't end with him,' Elwyn said, turning back to the crowd. 'Nothing we can do will root it out. But we have to protect each other from it. And from our short-sightedness.' Piety's brow was furrowed, and Elwyn thought he saw a dampness in her eyes, on her cheek. For a moment, it was just the two of them, eyes locked on each other. The crowd was silent. Elwyn's speech was over; he was never good at endings. His words just hung in the air. Then Piety began clapping. The rest of the audience joined in with some hesitation. 'Thank you,' Elwyn said. The journalists began to speak over each other, shouting out questions. Hestia stepped beside him on the platform.

'We have proof of what Elwyn said, along with several other illegal deals from the past decade,' she yelled over the noise. 'He is using a loophole to seize people's land by claiming that the current use is a threat to national security. This is blatantly false and has been padded by bribes to many local and national officials, whose names are listed here,' she said, handing some papers out to a journalist. 'My father's actions are not only illegal, but set a danger-ous precedent. We need you to hold him accountable.'

Her voice seemed to knock Rhoad out of whatever spell held him. He stood and limped quickly towards her, but she jumped away, handing out more papers to the journalists as she went. They scrambled for what she gave them as chaos began to grow in the crowd. The security guards whistled.

'We need to get out of here.' Hestia grabbed Elwyn's arm and pulled him off the stage. They got back into the car, but this time Hestia sat in the driver's seat. She started the engine, looking exhilarated and afraid.

'You know how to drive?' Elwyn asked.

'Just well enough.'

The car lurched forward, and as it did, hands pounded on Elwyn's window. He jumped in his seat, but seeing who it was, yelled for Hestia to stop. He opened the door.

'You're going home? Home to Badfish Creek?' Piety asked quickly, her face flushed.

'I have to,' Elwyn said, thinking she meant to tell him to stay. But she didn't.

'Let me come with you.'

# CHAPTER 31

# You Can't Return

HESTIA, ELWYN AND PIETY drove through the back hill roads along the river, which was dark as though it had swallowed the clouds. The streets near Liberty were well kept, clear of livestock and stray branches, but the ride felt bumpy to Elwyn, and they seemed to be going very fast. Any pleasure in the novelty of car travel had vanished with the urgency he felt in getting back to Badfish Creek. He held onto his seat. His heart was in his throat, and he kept turning around to see if they were being followed.

Even when they were far from town and got on the main road east from Liberty, Elwyn was looking behind them. They passed many little places where gasoline or a sandwich could be purchased, but they didn't stop. There were two tins of fuel in the back, and as for their stomachs, adrenalin was still flowing in their veins. For a while there was an energy in the car, but none of them spoke. There was just the sound of the engine, wind, and gravel crunching below them. Elwyn could hear his own heart pumping. Then the wink of a smile appeared on Hestia's face.

'We did it,' she said. And so they had. They had let the world know about Rhoad. Records had been handed over to the press. Elwyn had told his story. Slowly, feeling came back into Elwyn's limbs. Hestia's face was flushed, her eyes on the road ahead glistened. And Piety wore an expression Elwyn had never seen before. She had a dishevelled glow, like a smothered fire uncovered. She wasn't smiling, but she looked happy, and the look deepened as they drove on, farther and farther from town.

In the car, the world passed by quickly, but time moved slowly. The river wound out of view and the road became dimpled with holes. After a while the trees edging fat barley fields became more numerous, wilder, and then they swallowed the farms altogether. The smells of the forest crept in through the walls of the car, rich smells of loam and bark in humid air. Elwyn realised for the first time in his body – not just his mind – that he was going home. The eagerness he felt was almost painful.

'I remember the first time I came into the woods,' Piety said, interrupting Elwyn's thoughts. He was sitting beside Hestia in the front, and Piety was in the back, stretched across the seat and staring out the window. 'I was taking the train to tell your mother about Father's death. I had never travelled by train alone before, much less out into the woods, but I was devoted to the idea of duty, then, and that made me bold. People think of dutifulness as a meek, submissive thing, but just as often it's the opposite.' The road was very bumpy, now, and Hestia shifted gears to go slower; the shadowy branches passed more slowly overhead. 'I remember so clearly the moment the train passed from the fields into the forest. I became very nervous and wrung my gloves so much I damaged the seams. It seemed like a place without safety, and it scared me. The birds, the trees, the animals all appeared sinister. But everything looks different now.'

'Why did you come with us?' Elwyn asked.

Piety was quiet for a minute before she answered, looking out at the passing shadows. 'When you were a child, I sent you those letters because I thought I could help you. People my age are always thinking they are the ones who need to help everyone, fix everything. But you become afraid as you get older. Not in the way children are afraid – of the dark or monsters or spiders. People my age become afraid of the stupidest possible things someone can be afraid of. And when I saw you on that stage, you reminded me what it's like to be fearless.' Piety paused. 'And you reminded me of the things I always loved about my sister.'

'So you've come for some personal journey? To make yourself feel better?' Hestia said.

'You have every reason to be cynical,' Piety said. 'But the things that serve you when you are young are no good if you can't let go of them.' Hestia's eyes narrowed on the road. Elwyn was also looking straight ahead. All he could think about now was getting back to Badfish Creek, to find his family, to Whim. It seemed self-evident to him that you had to burn down old versions of yourself, like forests and fields sometimes needed to burn to make room for new growth.

But as they travelled deeper into the forest, the familiar smells, the movement of trees in the wind, stirred up feelings Elwyn couldn't ignore. Elwyn had often imagined the day he would return home. He'd be a little taller, handsomer, and very well dressed. He'd carry a sack of gifts over his shoulder. Gifts for everyone. Expensive ones. His mother would be proud. Girls would be after his attention. He'd have a whey-fed pig sent by rail, and they'd roast it over the coals for everyone, his mother getting the best cut. And all along the way, Elwyn would put generous tips into people's palms.

That was how it should have been. Instead, he was coming back with nothing but the tailored clothes on his back, their colours dimmed in the dull light. The pleasure of vanity was gone and so was the pleasure of pride. All that was left was his town. All that was left was to do was the right thing.

The three of them grew quiet, and the clouds in the sky thickened. The road through the woods was cheaply made – straight east with no attention given to the little Forester towns that dotted the landscape. Elwyn knew that they would eventually pass a mile or two south of Badfish Creek. How long it would take for them to reach this place, though, none of them knew. They had been driving all morning into the afternoon, and couldn't tell if the sun was getting lower or the clouds were getting darker, when a plink was heard on the windshield, and another and another. Then all at once, the rain fell in earnest, in sheets of heavy grey. Hestia slowed the car. They hardly moved, as Hestia squinted.

'We'll have to wait for it to pass,' she said, turning off the engine.

'Maybe we can drive through it. We can't be far away,' Elwyn said.

'I can't drive even a little ways in this weather.'

'Maybe I can.'

'We'll need to wait for it to pass.'

Elwyn's fingers drummed the leather siding. His stomach was empty, but he hardly noticed; it seemed hunger had defined his summer. He saw no value in patience. Every minute they sat unmoving in the car was another minute he wasn't home. He looked back at Piety. She had fallen asleep.

Then, Elwyn opened his door, and the sound and feel of the rain poured in.

'What are you doing?' Hestia asked, concern and scepticism in her voice.

'I'm going to take a look around. I can't get a sense of anything sitting in this car.'

'If you wander off, you're going to get lost.'

'I'm just going to take a look. I'll be back soon.'

He stepped out of the car, closing the door behind him and walking off the road into the woods. It felt good to be moving. Even through the thick leaves, the rain fell hard. Elwyn had trouble keeping it out of his eyes. Through his blurred vision, he thought he saw a trio of familiar trees in the distance, but when he neared, he was no longer sure.

Thunder growled overhead, but there was no visible lightning. Elwyn's fine, wet clothes clung uncomfortably as he pushed his way through the brush. Wild raspberry vines, their fruit now shrivelled, scratched his skin and poked holes through the cloth. Elwyn decided to turn around and go back to the car, but when he attempted it, he found Hestia was right: the rain had him all turned about. The sky was darkening, and the thunder deepened. He didn't know the way.

That was when he saw the clump of ripe elderberry bushes. It was one of the patches Whim used to visit, the one that made a perfect semicircle. It was a little far from town, but it was familiar. Elwyn was surprised by the effect it had on him, the way his knees felt weak. He set out, heart in his throat and tears in his eyes that he wiped away with the rain.

He pushed branches and brambles aside, moving so quickly, he didn't see the mud-slicked tracks until he was shoe-deep in them. The rain was letting up, but the sky was dimming into dusk. In the distance, he could see a grey strip of sky where the trees stopped. He thought he had gone the wrong way. A clearing meant a lake or pond. Elwyn decided he'd go there and get his bearings before trying to find his way back to the car.

But when Elwyn got to that clear place, there was no pond. Only a pile of felled familiar trees and the rubble of several houses, including his own. His heart pounded. He ran as well as he could over the slick earth, leaping over trunks and branches to the homes left standing, the homes he had visited so many times before. They were filled with people sheltering from the weather, the sounds of rain and the dampness of the air covering them. House after house was filled with people who hugged him, people he cried with. His sisters embraced him and, talking over each other, cried while telling him everything that had happened. But they didn't know where Whim was. Elwyn couldn't find who he was looking for.

## CHAPTER 32

# *The Girl and the Drake*

WHIM WOKE THE NEXT MORNING in the grey dawn with the first birds. Their chattering was confused, faded. They, too, had lost their nests. But their voices were beautiful nonetheless: the sweet cedar waxwing, conversational orioles, busy robins.

*Birds*, Aelred had often told Whim, *can tell you something.*

Whim turned on her side, towards the creek. When the rain started yesterday afternoon, she had taken shelter under a wide fallen log and chose to spend the night there on the bare ground rather than return home. The Moone house was still standing, but she couldn't bear to enter it. Her father's presence filled that place. On the ground, she was sore and damp, but at least she could breathe, open and shut her eyes. It felt good to be alone.

Along with her father, two of the workmen had been killed. The rest had fled. It was quiet, now, and on the creek, mallards were paddling in the early light. The sounds of the birds said nothing to Whim, least of all the mutterings of ducks. She felt, then, that the world itself had nothing to say to her. And even if it did, why should she listen? It had taken the things she loved from her. The ducks began to squabble over something or other, and a drake was chased out of the water, flying right over Whim's head. In that minute, she remembered something she had almost forgotten, a story March Wilder had once told her. She had been ten, and March was trying to amuse her while her father and Janie haggled over the price of sugar.

'Once there was a girl who had a magic drake,' March had said. 'Every night at sunset, the girl would take the drake to the creek and sing to him, and while she sang, the drake paddled through the water. Behind him, he left a trail of brilliant colours. When the colours faded, the fish multiplied, and the water became more abundant, and the town lived in prosperity along its banks.

'Until one day, when two thieves passed through by night. They were very hungry and seeing this fat, well-fed duck, they killed and ate it, leaving the bones beside their cooking fire. The girl found the bones there the next morning. But to the townspeople's surprise, at sunset the girl went out to the creek's edge and began to sing, even though her drake was not there to swim in the water. No colours came, no fish multiplied. The town didn't prosper as it once had. But each day at sunset, the girl still went down to the water and sang.

'Every day this continued. And then, a woman who had lost her child was crying in her home and she heard the girl singing. And the woman walked down to the bank and joined her, singing along. The next day, an old man who never married the woman he loved walked down and joined the song.

'Every day, another person would hear something in the girl's song and be reminded of their own grief. More and more people came down to the banks of the river, until the town stood empty.'

That was the end of the story. It had made Whim sad when she heard it as a child, the loss of her mother still visible on Aelred's face. But recalling the story as she watched the ducks on the water – the stench of mildew on her unwashed clothes, hunger in her belly, hollowness in her chest – it cast a sliver of light.

That was when Whim heard the bee. It flew right above her, hovering by her nose. Whim winced as she got to her feet and followed as the bee skidded away. It stopped here and there to land, disappearing and reappearing on its path away from the water. More and more bees joined it.

'Finchy?' Whim said. The bees swarmed a bush in the distance, and as she approached, Whim saw that their boxes of hives had been set up amongst the gnarled branches. And there was an odd little shelter, too, set up beside it. A shelter made of familiar tablecloths and lace curtains.

'Finchy?' Whim ran. 'Finchy?' When she reached the shelter, she drew back the lace door. Crouched in the darkness was the old woman holding a heavy stick.

'Don't you dare think I'm a coward,' she whispered, small eyes red, leathery face defiant. 'My bees. I had to protect my bees.'

'Finchy. . .' Whim began, emotion welling up in her.

'Hush,' she said. 'Do you have ears, girl?'

Whim was quiet. And at first she heard nothing but the bees, the red-winged blackbirds, the quarrelling squirrels. Then, faintly, in the distance, she heard it. Voices, two voices, calling for Elwyn.

Elwyn.

Whim ran before Finchy could stop her. She only half-heard the hoarse whispers of the old woman ordering her to come back. She couldn't. She tried to shout Elwyn's name, but her throat wouldn't open. She just ran towards the voices, ran with weak knees.

The voices grew louder and louder, then stopped entirely. Whim looked around, recognising where she was immediately as the place where she first heard the trucks go by, the trucks that had started everything. The weight of the memory froze her in place. She almost thought she could hear them still, the ghosts of the automobiles still living inside her. But then a voice stirred Whim from her recollection.

'Quick,' the voice said. 'It might be a demolition crew, and we can't just let them by. Help me drag this, in case. It will block the road, at least for a while.'

Whim peered through the bushes to see Hestia Rhoad and a woman who looked like a sharp and slender version of Mirth Bramble. They were dragging a log, their hair dishevelled and their good clothes creased and dirty-hemmed. Whim held back, keeping hidden, watching.

Hestia and the woman dragged the log across the puddle-and-mud-covered road, then hid themselves on the other side.

By the time they finished, Whim realised that it wasn't her imagination recalling the sound of vehicles. Coming down the road was a yellow truck, large and splattered with dirt. Whim ducked deeper down into the bushes, hiding from what she thought could be officials coming to check on progress at the mining site. Her heart was in her throat.

The truck stopped when it reached the log. As Whim expected, a man stepped out to move it, but when she saw his face, her breath caught in her chest. It was Cronus Rhoad, his sleeves rolled up. He was handsomer than his newspaper pictures and also fiercer. In that moment, she saw more of the man who traded along the Messipi than the man who went to fundraisers and gave speeches. Rhoad struggled with the log, cursing. When he finally succeeded and turned back to the truck, Hestia walked out in front of it.

'Out of the way,' he said, brushing the bark from his hands.

'I won't,' Hestia said.

At the sound of his daughter's voice, he looked up. Rhoad was silent for a moment. His shoulders relaxed with what looked like relief before anger returned to his face. That look of relief surprised Whim, and maybe it should have made her feel some small measure of pity or understanding. Instead, the love she saw briefly on his face made her livid. Who was Rhoad to feel fatherly love? Rhoad, who had taken it from her. She searched the ground around her and found a sharp stone.

'Get in the truck, Hestia,' Rhoad finally said.

'No.'

'Do you have any idea what you've done? I have lost everything. Everything, Hestia. My reputation is destroyed, my future is precarious, my wife is furious. This is not the time to cross me.'

'I'll get in the truck with you if you turn around. If you turn yourself over to the law and face the consequences of what you've done.'

'Get into the truck,' he said, face turning red again, grabbing his daughter by the arm. Hestia struggled, but she wasn't as strong as her father. Whim's stomach churned.

But then Elwyn's aunt ran out of the woods, a thick fallen branch in her hand. 'Let her go,' she said, and when he didn't listen, she sent the branch down onto Rhoad's shoulder. He dropped Hestia's arm, cursing.

'You don't have to do this,' Hestia said to her father, whose face was screwed up in pain. 'When you were young you had to take everything you could get your hands on, fight for it. But it's not like that any more. We have enough. We don't need this sand mine.'

'You still think that's what this is all about, Hestia? About me? About greed? Have you listened to a word I've said? I'm saving this country.' Rhoad shook his head. Tears of fury stood in Hestia's eyes, and Piety stood beside her with a hand on Hestia's shoulder. 'You've seen nothing but the glossed surface of the world. We're living in a land of abundance, but we're crawling through it like ants. The Collective should never have become this backward, forgotten place, and it will never change unless someone changes it. That mine will be built. I have people working for me. I can lie low and manage things from a distance. It's not ideal, but at least this country will keep moving forward.'

'So you're just going to sit around while people's lives are destroyed? Hide out in one of your friends' remote, fancy lake houses and hope that the law won't catch up with you?'

'Of course it won't. No one with power cares about this, Hestia. It doesn't affect them, so they have no reason to pursue it. You'll see. This has cost me time, but in several years, I'll be able to run again, and I'll lift this country to its proper place.'

'And on whose back are you going build this new country?' Hestia said. 'There will be consequences for you. I won't let you get away with this.'

'You think you are a righteous rebel, but you're just a sheltered, spoilt girl. Of course there will be casualties,' Rhoad said. 'If you had ever spent time out on the land, you would know that the old grass sometimes needs to be burned away for the new grass to thrive.'

Anger surged in Whim and she snuck forward and swiftly punctured one of the truck's tyres with the stone. It hissed, a sound like a snake. Rhoad lunged at her, but before he could reach her, she punctured another tyre. He grabbed her by the arm, face violet, and before Whim knew what she was doing, she had the stone poised above her head, ready to bring down onto his skull.

She saw a flash of fear in Rhoad's eyes and it satisfied her. It satisfied her? Before this summer, Whim had been a stranger to anger. Now she was consumed by it. That some things had to die so others could flourish was a fact; Rhoad had come this far because he accepted that to get what you want, there had to be casualties, but Whim wasn't Rhoad. She couldn't accept cruel terms of life with the ease he did. Hurting him would not bring her father back. It wouldn't put the fallen trees back in their places or put houses back together, piece by broken piece.

Her arm wavered, just a little, and when Rhoad used the opportunity to grab her wrist and push her to the ground, she wasn't afraid nor even surprised. What surprised her was what happened next: as she lay on the ground, one of Rhoad's hands around her wrist, the other raised to strike her, Hestia threw herself onto her father, her arm wrestling his.

'Get off, Hestia,' Rhoad said. But Hestia didn't. Then Elwyn's aunt joined her, but it wasn't they who caused Rhoad to suddenly stumble sideways. He clutched his hand to his head. Whim didn't understand what had happened. Hestia, too, looked around, confused.

Then Elwyn pushed his way through the brush and onto the road, sling in hand. His eyes fell on his friend and didn't leave.

'Whim,' Elwyn said. 'I told you to practise with that sling.' And he smiled, but it wasn't the boyish smile she was used to. It was a face that was altered in a way she couldn't quantify, but that warmed her, in a day that was damp and grey.

# CHAPTER 33

# Gashes

THE NIGHT BEFORE and all through the morning, Elwyn had been lost to himself. The house he had grown up in had been demolished; the town was hardly recognisable. But seeing his best friend made him feel at home. The glow Whim had when Elwyn last saw her had gone. There was an ashiness to her skin and hair. But despite that, seeing her still brought a freshness, like it was spring.

The stone had just grazed Rhoad's head, but it left a gash in its wake. Elwyn wanted them to take him to Badfish Creek, not just to treat the wound, but to show him the place he nearly destroyed. He thought if they could show Rhoad where his house had been, the path Samuel Bramble first took to get there, the now-fallen trees that had watched it all, Rhoad might have some sort of change of heart.

'It's the only way we can make this end well,' Elwyn said. 'Having someone like Rhoad on our side, to help us rebuild, to protect us from having this ever happen again – it's exactly what we need.' Rhoad was quiet as Hestia and Piety used ropes from the truck to bind his hands and legs. He didn't struggle. His clothes were still unrumpled somehow, his face civil in its silence. But as Elwyn spoke, Hestia, Whim and Piety guided Rhoad into the back of the car, watching him shrewdly.

'It's a bad idea,' Hestia said.

Elwyn objected, but Whim spoke gently. 'Your optimism is something we're going to need, Elwyn. But not for him.' Rhoad was sitting silently in the back of the car Hestia had driven the day before. He knew when it was worth speaking and when to keep quiet. Looking at him there, Elwyn recalled the first time he saw Cronus Rhoad. It was in a house full of light.

'I'm going to drive him home. To the jail,' Hestia said, filling the tank with gas and testing the lock of the door, the security of the ropes.

'You're going back to Liberty?' Elwyn said.

'I have to talk to the newspapers, lawyers. My father has to answer to the courts for what he's done.'

'I know but. . . I thought you'd stay here with us.'

'I have to do this, Elwyn. If you want to help with the case against him, you know where to find me.' Elwyn's face fell, but Hestia, in a rare moment of affection, wrapped Elwyn in a hug, then turned to Whim and embraced her, too. 'And I hope you *do* come, sometime. We could use witnesses at the trial.'

'Well? Are you ready?' Hestia said, turning to Piety, who had been quiet for some time. But Piety shook her head. 'I'm not coming,' she said. So Hestia drove down the muddy road with no one but her father, tied up in the back.

'Well,' Elwyn said. 'I guess all that's left for us is to go home, for now."

'Did you hear what Rhoad said? About having things set in motion?' Whim looked west down the road.

'Hestia won't let anything more happen to Badfish Creek. She's smart. She knows how to do everything,' Elwyn said, and he believed it. But below that confidence were his own worries. There was a future that was now blank.

He held out his hand and Whim took it. He squeezed Whim's hand and she squeezed back.


Piety threw herself into the work of rebuilding with a Mirth-like vigour. She raked and dug through the ground for people's belongings. She sorted and searched for lumber. The only break she took was to put a postscript in the letter Elwyn sent to his mother. He had written to tell her that he was safe, Badfish Creek would be okay, and she should come home. Piety simply added, in her small, crisp hand, that she was eager to see her sister as well.

But the letter never reached Mirth. The day after it was sent, a voice was heard over the morning goose-chatter. Elwyn had just woken, his body stiff with work after weeks of disuse. The sun was out, dew was underfoot, and the droplets of water vapour sparkled in the yellow light of August.

'Elwyn!' the voice called again. Then Elwyn could see her, pulling a heavy cart, flanked on either side by Teilo and Loew. 'Elwyn. You have some explaining to do.' Elwyn stepped out onto the path she walked, and Mirth set down the cart. His pants were dirty and dew-soaked, but his mother didn't even glance at them. 'I read what you did in a paper, and I figured I'd find you here. You can be so reckless.' Mirth's voice was choked with anger, but also with relief. Before she could finish, Elwyn walked towards her, and she wrapped her arms around him, pulling her son to her as if he were still a young boy, not one her own height, nearly grown. Elwyn could feel the thick, warm tears on her cheek. Her shoulders began to shake. 'I'm so glad you're safe,' she said. 'I'm so glad you're home.'

'I'm glad, too,' Loew said, wrapping his arms around them both.

'Mam!' Enid said, running towards them. Her usually laughing eyes were as full of tears as her mother's as she joined the embrace. Then Neste came. Soon all six of them were wrapped up together, a bundle of arms, torsos and wet cheeks.

'Allun and Dewey will be coming in a few days,' Mirth said when they finally separated, wiping her cheeks. 'They were with Posy's family and couldn't get going as quickly as we did.'

'No one could get going as fast as we did,' Loew said. 'Mam walked full speed all the way here. We didn't stop once. She had us sleep on top of the cart at night while she pulled us, and only napped a bit during the day.'

'Loew,' Mirth scolded.

'She never slept for long. She was worried we weren't fast enough or safe. She had nightmares—'

'Enid, Neste – you girls take Loew and Teilo to get some rest. There's a lot to be done, and you won't be any use if you don't get some sleep.'

'They can sleep at Whim's house,' Elwyn said. 'She's probably there now. She'll want to see you all.'

'Where is Aelred?' Mirth asked after the siblings started down towards the marsh. 'I need to speak to him. To apologise.'

'Aelred died,' Elwyn said. The words felt wrong, like they didn't belong to him. Mirth was looking after her children as they walked away.

'Poor girl,' she said quietly. The wrinkles on her face had grown more pronounced. 'And what about our home?' she said after a few moments. They left the cart and Elwyn walked with his mother along the path through the thick, wooded part of the forest to the place where the soil had been torn, houses toppled, trees felled. Mirth went where their house had been, and crouched over a piece of wood that had been part of their floor, smoothed by generations of feet.

She stared at that piece of wood for what seemed like a long time before her large shoulders began to heave. Elwyn went and knelt beside her. He was unaccustomed to his mother crying and didn't know what to say.

'It was your father's house. It was the place he grew up, and when I walked those floors, cooked on the stove his mother cooked at, I remembered him,' she said, her voice lilting. 'My parents disowned me when I married him, so his family was my family. *He* was my family. And now. . .' Mirth wiped the tears with her calloused hands. When she looked up, she saw her sister on the other side of the clearing. Piety didn't see her; she was too focused on the collecting and sorting of wood she was tending to. Mirth's body went tense.

'Aunt Piety wanted to come back with me for a while. She helped us. . .' Elwyn began, but his mother didn't seem to hear. She stood slowly and strode towards her sister with large, deliberate steps.

When Piety saw her sister, she straightened. 'I didn't know if you'd want me here. But I came just the same. I came to help you,' she said.

Mirth's face was stony. She took a step closer, her body imposing next to her sister's.

Then Mirth opened her arms. The two sisters embraced, and didn't let go for a long time. They were inseparable the rest of the summer. Where one went, so did the other.

# CHAPTER 34

# *What Was Found*

ELWYN TRUSTED HESTIA, and he was right. Within weeks, she had all the deeds turned back to the citizens of Badfish Creek, and a law enforcement officer was stationed in the town to ensure no developers came to work on the mine until Rhoad was tried and matters were settled.

Rhoad's trial, like Aelred's, was a constant feature in the newspapers. People were coming forward almost daily with new revelations of Rhoad's transgressions: bribery, land-grabbing, coercion. As a result, they didn't need Elwyn and Whim as witnesses. The trial went on smoothly without them, resulting in not only five years in jail for Rhoad, but also reparations to be paid to the people he had defrauded in the past. Hestia wrote that her mother was furiously funnelling funds into different accounts while their house in Liberty was being seized along with several other properties questionably obtained. Dealers spent the day taking down the mirrors and crystal lamps, wrapping up the gold-leaf tea sets. It would all be sold and the profits scattered. Letitia Rhoad left for St Louis as soon as she could, but Hestia stayed in the house while it was being emptied. It was the first time she enjoyed being there.

Elwyn and Whim were too busy to bother with the truck whose tyres had been slashed. It sat forgotten on the side of the road, Virginia creeper growing over its hood. A couple weeks after the trial, Hestia arrived. She spent two weeks visiting, helping raise the walls of the Alfin house and splitting logs for shingles. Teilo doted on her goat.

She spent some time helping Whim with the ongoing elderberry harvest as well, her hands purple from separating berries from the stems, but it was the rough work she liked best. And that was how Elwyn would remember her – tireless, wild-haired, swinging an axe. A dozen or so Badfishians walked with her to the truck when it was time to go (she had brought patches for the tyres with her). Dewey was irritated that an automobile had been there the whole time and no one had made use of it, but Mirth told him to hush. Hestia was sent on her way with one of Finchy's bottles of mead, a bundle of dried venison, and a small pouch Elwyn had made with a letter inside. They all waved as she drove away.

'Good riddance,' Enid said as Hestia drove out of sight. 'A person can only take being showed up by a bossy Hill girl for so long.'

'Nonsense. She was a help to us,' Mirth said. Teilo was next to her, laughing as Willoughby ate leaves out of his hand. Hestia had left her goat with him, knowing her pet would be appreciated and well cared for. She said she'd be back to visit him soon.

Long after the truck drove out of sight and everyone turned back to Badfish Creek, Elwyn still looked down the road after Hestia. Summer was over. His aunt had left the week before, the birds had finished their mating songs, and the last August storm had passed. The day suddenly felt very quiet, full of the smell of the nuts that fell from the trees.

Elwyn stayed there for some time. Then, instead of turning back towards town, Elwyn went off in the other direction. He wanted to be alone, and so he walked through the woods downstream along the creek, moving quickly but quietly, observed by the muskrats and cranes. There in the reeds along the bank, Elwyn saw something out of the corner of his eye: a bit of polished wood. He lifted it from the tangle of grasses, wiped mud from its belly. It was his box. The object that used to contain his most treasured things.

Inside it was just the same. There were the letters from his aunt, the arrowhead, the coin. It was like time hadn't passed inside those small wooden walls. Elwyn looked at them, felt the surfaces cautiously. He palmed the coin, opened one of the letters. Then the wind picked up and sent an envelope flying. Elwyn chased after it, finally catching up when it got stuck in a wild raspberry patch. He put it back with the others and closed the lid.

When he got home, Elwyn knew he would clean the box and return it to its place under his bed. But this was only out of sentiment. The things inside no longer meant much to Elwyn. It was like they belonged to someone else, someone he had hardly known.

October was around the corner, and as always, change was in the air. The walnut trees were turning yellow. The sun, too, was yellowing, the acorns growing heavy. As Elwyn returned from his walk, he could hear Finchy humming as she tended her bees, his sisters laughing through the kitchen window of the Moone house by the creek as they set out breakfast.

Elwyn would wash the box and wash his hands. Then he would take his seat at the table.

PUSHKIN CHILDREN'S BOOKS

We created Pushkin Children's Books to share tales from different languages and cultures with younger readers, and to open the door to the wide, colourful worlds these stories offer.

From picture books and adventure stories to fairy tales and classics, and from fifty-year-old bestsellers to current huge successes abroad, the books on the Pushkin Children's list reflect the very best stories from around the world, for our most discerning readers of all: children.